Darkness in the Art

Prelude of *"The Tales of Albion Trilogy"*

Darkness in the Art

Prelude of *"The Tales of Albion Trilogy"*

R.J. Pommarane

Cover Art and Illustrations by
Heather Lewis

Sunfyre Books, LLC

First Printing: 2014

ISBN: 978-0-9903709-1-8 (paperback); 978-0-9903709-2-5 (eBook)

Sunfyre Books, LLC
PO Box 12024
Portland, OR 97212
www.sunfyrebooks.com

Cover Art: Copyright © 2014 by Heather Lewis
Author Website: www.rjpommarane.com

This one is for my mother:
Thanks for all your encouragement and support.

Acknowledgments

If I thanked everyone involved in the long development of this mythical history these acknowledgements would go on for pages. Therefore, I would briefly like to thank Tara, Jackson, David, and Randi for providing the inspiration for many of my characters. I want to thank all the authors who have written about Atlantis before me and, most of all, I want to show my appreciation to my beloved Kevin. Without you I would never have come this far.

Table of Contents

Preface

A note on the stories contained herein:

From Plato to Sir Francis Bacon, from Herodotus to Marion Zimmer Bradley, the myth of Atlantis has captivated the hearts of writers and readers alike. I am no exception. As a young man, I fantasized about what the world of Atlantis would've been like. Who was the ruler and which gods did they worship? With no real answers to these questions, I set out to fashion the ancient world from the depths of my imagination. As a fan of fairy tales and magical adventures, I knew I wanted my Atlantis to be filled with witches and wizards, gods and elves, and all the other things that man has dreamt up to keep their fantasies alive in a world that values materialism in the absence of dreaming.

I have superimposed a great deal of pagan imagery and ceremony onto these stories but they are not meant to serve as a spiritual handbook or a condemnation of any other faith. These are works of fiction, meant to take the reader on a journey through the fabricated history of a lost civilization struggling with some of the same issues that plague our own societies today. The only issue I mean to address openly with these stories is one of choice: each character is faced with a choice during the course of their trials and tribulations. The choices they make determine the future events of this series of short stories, driving them to defend the powers of the light or to fall from grace and embrace the Darkness in the Art...

Ages of Albion

The Age of the Old Gods
1 EI – 979 EI
The Age of the Elfin Empresses
1 AI – 503 AI
The First Reign of the Black Prince
503 AI – 794 AI
The Time of the Wyt Kings
1 UI – 23 UI
The Tyranny of the Witch-Queen
23 UI – 32 UI
The Second Reign of the Black Prince
32 UI – 65 UI
The Regency of the Wyt Robes
65 UI
The Age of the Divine Matriarchy
65 UI – 86 UI

The Stages of the Art

Adepts

Adepts are the lowest level of practitioners of the Art and a man from any background may join these ranks. Adepts practice the Art as it is written in the General Annals once present in the Corr Libraries across Albion. These ritualistic spells require Adepts to gather in Covens, pooling their energy to accomplish powerful feats of magic. During the time of the Elfin Empresses and the caste systems of man, there were no Adepts. After the rise of the Wyt Kings, the Adepts flourished, only to be eradicated under the rule of the orthodox Divine Matriarchs. There are still some Adepts in the realms of Ikaria and the Wynterlande Forest but they are few.

Priests

Priests are the intermediary level of practitioners of the Art. Any man who vows himself to the service of the Old Gods may become a priest and begin studying the Secret Annals only present in the Old Temples. Priests are able to practice the Art solitarily with great potency but they do not readily cast spells or perform rituals for fear of disrupting the balance of nature. Priests were numerous during the reign of the Elfin Empresses and the Wyt Kings but their numbers have been drastically reduced under the rule of orthodox Divine Matriarchs of Atlantis. Priests and priestesses still practice the Art in Ikaria and the Wynterlande Forest but they are few in number.

Wizards

Wizards are the greatest practitioners of the Art and only those born of the ancient bloodlines of the wizarding clans may learn the secret ways of their ancestors. Wizards are the only practitioners who utilize the craft of Spirit-Magic to create talismans that greatly enhance and focus their magic. Wizards belong to six different clans (Wyts, Greys, Browns, Greens, Reds, and Blues) and practice the Art according to their Order. The clans were always prominent in the ancient days of Albion but have been nearly exterminated by the Divine Matriarchs. Those who remain fight towards the reunification of the clans and the restoration of the ancient ways of Albion at all costs.

The Wizarding Clans

Wyt Robes

Wizards of the Wyt Robes are servants of Raanon, the God of Light. They dwelt upon the Great Mountain in the Atland until they were exterminated by the Divine Matriarchs for crimes against Atlantis. The Wyt Robes utilize moonstone rings as their sacred talismans and possess mastery over all forms of light. Wyt Robes shave their heads and wear the symbols of the Sacred Feminine and the Sacred Masculine tattooed to their scalps. They were considered the greatest of the wizarding clans until they met their untimely end.

Grey Robes

Wizards of the Grey Robes are servants of Ragnar the Fallen, the God of Twilight. They dwelt within the Caves of a Thousand Tears in the west of the Atland until after their master, calling himself the Black Prince, was defeated by the Wyt Robes. The Grey Robes then claimed the Ruined City of Tansapar as their new home. Grey Robes utilize diamond tipped wands as their sacred talismans and possess mastery over darkness and shadows. Grey Robes have split into two groups: those working with the clans and those fighting them.

Brown Robes

Wizards of the Brown Robes are servants of Anara, the Goddess of Mountains. They dwelt upon the Great Mountain in the Atland alongside the Wyt Robes until leaving during the reign of the Nerys. They then went to live under the protection of the Elfin Lady of the Green City in Ikaria. Brown Robes use quartz amulets as their sacred talismans and possess mastery over the air. Brown Robes wear their hair in tonsures and tattoo the symbols of the Sacred Masculine and Sacred Feminine on their arms after initiation into their order.

Green Robes

Wizards of the Green Robes are servants of Ahtarrah, Goddess of the Groves. They dwelt in the Marshland Forest of the Atland until exiled by the authority of the Divine Matriarchs. They then went to live under the protection of the Elfin Lady of the Green City in Ikaria to await a day when they might return to their ancestral home. Green Robes utilize emerald-tipped oak staffs as their sacred talismans and possess mastery over all things that grow from the earth. Green Robes wear full beards and long hair and prefer to remain isolated.

Red Robes

Wizards of the Red Robes are servants of Annatar, the God of Fire. They dwelt in the Sun Pyramid of Lemuria until driven out by the followers of the One God, when they journeyed to Ikaria seeking the protection of the Elfin Lady of the Green City. Red Robes utilize ruby-hilted swords as their sacred talismans and possess mastery over heat and flames. For a time, it seemed the Red Robes would follow the Greys into the darkness but, under the leadership of the famed Dairu Ral, they turned back towards the light and remain united with the clans.

Blue Robes

Wizards of the Blue Robes are servants of Galos, the God of the Sea. They dwelt upon the Ennis Isles until the rise of the Witch-Queen when they were driven into exile, seeking out the protection of the Elfin Lady of the Green City in Ikaria. Blue Robes utilize sapphire-topped scepters as their sacred talismans and possess mastery over waves and water. The Blue Robes claim to be the oldest of the wizarding clans which has been a point of contention amongst the clans for centuries, causing heated arguments and outright fights.

The Old Gods

Ahtarrah, Goddess of the Groves.

Amhir, God of the Winds.

Anara, Goddess of the Mountains.

Annatar, God of Fire.

Araset, God of the Dead.

Audrid, Goddess of Love.

Danu, Goddess of Storms.

Eathir, God of Youths.

Galos, God of the Sea.

Karenthir, God of the Harvest.

Loryn, God of the Frosts.

Lyra, Goddess of Beauty.

Maru, Goddess of the Waxing Moon.

Narenna, Goddess of the Waning Moon.

Nerwyn, God of the Dark Waters.

Nora, Goddess of the Hearth.

Ortheon, God of the Forge.

Raanon, God of Light.

Ragnar, God of Twilight.

Selena, Goddess of the Full Moon.

Tsira, Goddess of the Dark Moon.

Tyrena, Goddess of Elders.

Varos, God of Wisdom.

Yana, Goddess of Virgins.

Tsira and the One God

Faced with the unchecked and violent nature of men, the Old Gods sat in council, deciding to withdraw from the living world into that hidden realm beyond the land in the shadows, that Otherworld where mortal spirits go to rest after the years of their life have passed. Araset, god of the dead, had always dwelt in the Otherworld, in a grand palace set upon the tallest mountain in the mirror world. It was there in the Otherworld that the Old Gods made their home, except for a single defiant voice who determined he would remain in Albion to help shape a better future for men.

Theis, god of life, had always been a champion of men. When the other gods and goddesses spoke ill of their lackluster progenies, Theis came readily to their defense. It was natural for him to remain behind and, despite their objections, the Old Gods did not try to stop him. They departed and he remained, going to live amongst the tribes of men to instill peace into their violent hearts. Most shunned him, some threatened him with violence but, in the east, upon the isles of Lemuria he found a following. They worshipped him as their only deity, the living manifestation of divinity, and they called him the One God. They forsook all the ancient practices of their tribe, including the practice of the Art, and followed the One God towards a new way of living where loyalty became of the most paramount importance. They were taught to love their neighbor and to give even when they had nothing. They were washed in sacred waters blessed by the hands of the One God and came to his temple in Lemuria to hear him speak. All who saw him fell under his spell. Soon, the number of the congregants in his temple had grown considerably. He had the power to push his religion across the Eastern Sea and into the Atland but his doctrines were met with cold cynicism and irreverent disdain by the leaders of the Atlandish tribes living in warring factions throughout their homeland.

For many years the Old Gods lived apart, each following their own future. In time the gods and goddesses gathered in council to discuss a pressing matter foreseen by the four goddesses known collectively as the Daughters of the Moon.

The Daughters of the Moon were the greatest of the Old Goddesses, standing above all others in grace and prestige, save the youngest sister, Tsira. Tsira was the goddess of the dark moon and the Old Gods worshipped light above all other things. The eldest sister, Narenna, was the goddess of the Waning Moon, then came Selena, goddess of the Full Moon, and finally, Maru goddess of the Waxing Moon. These three sisters were known communally as the Triple Goddess, while Tsira was an outcast unloved by her sisters and openly disrespected by the other gods and goddesses. A dark hatred began to grow in her heart as she was ignored by her sisters and the others. She took to sitting alone in the darkness and contemplating the course of her future. In a way, she envied Theis for his defiance and determination to forge his own path. But where Theis' destiny was fueled by his compassion and love for men, Tsira's future would be forged by her anger and resentment towards her peers and loved ones.

The sisters had been meditating for weeks under the light of the sunless stars at the edge of the Otherworld when they were confronted with a terrible vision that shook them to their core. The sisters saw Theis' influence grow to such an extent that his power became absolute in the living world but, what truly alarmed them was that such power would one day drive the One God to madness and, in his hysteria, he would unmake Albion by merging the three worlds.

"And you are sure it was Theis you saw in this vision?" asked Anara, goddess of the grove.

"Who else could it be?" asked Galos, god of the sea.

"It could have been one of us," said Ragnar, god of twilight, "the events of this vision took place hundreds of years in the future...how can we know one of us won't bring this darkness upon the living world?"

"Because we are here," replied Annatar, god of fire, "we have made our home far from Albion and our power even now fades from the living world...our dominion is this Land of the Dead and it is here we shall stay, even until the final days when the three worlds collide..."

"Not all of us," said Maru, "someone must return to the living world and bring an end to Theis' dominion before he grows too strong."

"We will not send you," replied Nerwyn, god of the dark waters, "you and Selena and Narenna are far too important.

"I will go," said Tsira whose position amongst her sisters had always been intensely unimportant.

"And what can you do, Tsira?" asked Audrid, goddess of love.

"I will wrap him in shadows and deliver him here at your feet. Then we shall decide what will become of him as a group," replied Tsira.

"Fine...you will return forthwith to Albion and deal with this One God," said Raanon, god of light, "bring him here so we may discuss the outcome of this vision."

Tsira left that night, crossing the River Lethe and passing through the mists, arriving on the southern slopes of the mountains in the Atland. Tsira knew that Theis had established his holy kingdom far in the east and she was astonished to see Temples of the One God in the Atland as she made her way towards the distant sea. She called the western wind to carry her across the water to Lemuria and found Theis at the altar in his golden citadel, around which the city of Yarra had risen. He looked upon Tsira and knew why she had come. He too had seen the vision of the future but believed it could not be him. He would never be driven to madness by the adoration of men. He loved mankind greatly and would never abide their suffering.

"I know you have seen what I have seen," said Theis.

"And what is it that you have seen?" asked Tsira.

"I saw the silhouette of a god standing upon thousands of corpses as the three worlds merged into one," said Theis, "I saw the absolute power of this god as he held something in his right hand and something in his left. But it could not have been me...I could never be tempted into corruption."

"I know your love for men is strong in this moment but it could easily turn to hatred, given the proper circumstances...we cannot risk this vision becoming a reality. It would surely destroy this world that is yours, and the world that is ours."

"What do you mean to do to me?" asked Theis.

"You will return to the Otherworld with me and answer for your shortcomings."

"But I have yet committed no crime."

"You are not meant to be punished. We simply want you to forsake this world as you should have when we left six centuries ago...if you stay here the future we have both seen will most assuredly come to pass."

Theis meant to accompany Tsira back to the Otherworld straightaway but as they prepared to forever leave behind the golden citadel, he began to have his doubts.

"I need but one more day, Tsira," he said sadly, "let me remain here until the morning sun rises over the walls of my citadel, that I may properly say goodbye to my Tetrarchs..."

Tsira was more sympathetic than she should've been and agreed to allow him one more day. When she went to collect him the next morning he had disappeared, having left Yarra under the cover of night for parts unknown. Tsira was immensely frustrated as she called upon the shadows to hunt him down and drag him back to her on his knees. Her temper got the better of her and an air of apathy began to overtake her face. She was hardened by her determination and was adamant she would not fail to fulfill her mission.

Tsira's motives became apparent as she sat there waiting for the shadows to deliver her news of the One God's whereabouts. She no longer feigned a desire to be the champion of the Old Gods and deliver Theis to their waiting arms. She took on a terrible persona as she ordered men about and inflicted upon them terrible punishments should they disobey her commands. The darkness of her fear turned her evil. It took the shadows weeks to locate Theis. They found him hiding in the high and treacherous Norn Mountains near the ices of the far north. Tsira wasted no time, calling upon the wind to carry her like a storm cloud to those mountains, to a deep cavern overlooking the icy sea. Theis was hiding in the darkness like a child fearing punishment from a harsh parent.

"I knew you would find me," he said.

"If you knew I would come for you then why did you run?"

"Because I don't wish to leave...I have made a home here. More and more men flock to my temples each day, looking upon me as both god and king. I have never felt such power..."

"You reveal yourself at last," said Tsira, "your love is not for men but for the power you wield over them."

"That is not true."

"Enough of this," snapped Tsira, calling the shadows to wrap themselves around Theis like chains. He struggled against their strength but was unable to break free. He looked at Tsira with sad eyes before the shadows overtook him completely and he was swallowed by the darkness, followed shortly thereafter by Tsira herself. They were standing in endless nothing stretching out in all directions like a universe without stars. Theis felt weak as Tsira came to stand beside him, her face full of hatred and her eyes changed from blue to the color of blood.

"This is not the Otherworld," said Theis, "Am I not meant to stand before the others and answer for my future sins?"

"You will answer only to me," replied Tsira.

"What has happened to you?"

"I am tired of being insulted because I am the mistress of the darkness," said Tsira, "I have been waiting for the opportunity to seek you out, to try a new kind of magic I created here in this void."

Tsira produced a beautiful golden amulet shaped like a teardrop, with a large and flawless diamond at its center, from the pocket of her robes. It hung from a long golden chain and had ancient godly runes etched on its front and back. She looked at it the way a mother looks at her favorite child as she flicked the chain with her fingers.

"Do you like my necklace?" she asked.

"It's very beautiful," replied Theis stubbornly.

"It sure is," laughed Tsira before chanting in a dark and terrible language Theis had never heard before.

"Hala nephtari azmal argan…firi kiliri azmar kahn…"

Theis felt a terrible pain in his chest before falling into the nothingness, shrieking from indescribable agony as his soul was ripped from his immortal body, appearing above him as an orb of pure white light shining like a star in the heart of the darkness. Tsira reached out and grabbed his soul like a marble, pushing it into the diamond of her amulet. The orb disappeared as the diamond began to emit a dull orange glow, fused with the One God's mighty powers. Without his soul, Theis' body faded, forever becoming one with the nothingness of the void. Tsira looked down at the amulet gripped tightly in her hand and smiled a monstrous grin. She had discovered the true power of spirit-magic and intended to turn it against those gods and goddesses who held her as inferior to them. But even as she began to slip the necklace over her head a giant disincarnate hand reached into the void and grabbed her by the neck, yanking her out of the darkness of her own creation with the force of a hurricane hitting a shallow coast.

Tsira found herself standing before the other gods and goddesses in the Palace of the Dead at the far reaches of the Otherworld. The gods and goddesses were assembled, sitting upon their thrones, each looking down upon her with disdain in their eyes. She was especially outraged by the looks of disgust adorning her sisters' faces. It was they who had made her the goddess of the dark moon and now they were meaning to punish her for that very reason.

"You were meant to bring Theis back to us so that we might ask him of this future where he becomes a tyrant," said Annatar.

"Where is he, Tsira?" added Narenna, "Why is he not standing here before us as he should be?"

"Something tells me you already know the answer to that question," smiled Tsira.

"We are aware of what you have done," said Karenthir, god of the harvest, "Now how can it be undone?"

"It cannot be undone," hissed Tsira as the diamond amulet containing Theis' soul was seized from her by Ragnar, god of twilight.

"You must be punished for this unthinkable crime," said Annatar.

"We must pass judgment," added Narenna.

"You will have to pay the ultimate price," said Karenthir.

The gods and goddesses sat in council for several days while Tsira was locked within her chambers at the top of the tallest tower in the Otherworld. When she was brought again before her peers, she was even more defiant and malevolent than before. She glared at Annatar and her sisters before turning on Ragnar, seated upon a throne of ivory.

"What have you done with my amulet?" she hissed.

"It is somewhere beyond your reach," replied Ragnar.

Tsira looked like she would murder each of the gods and goddesses as her face turned pale and her eyes glowed red. She looked more monster than woman as her beauty faded, giving way to a harsh and cold face contorted by fear and hatred.

"We have decided upon your punishment," said Annatar.

"You will be stripped of your living body," continued Maru, "and your spirit shall be bound to the black water of a deep well until you are given the virtue of a warrior youth…then your flesh will be remade, but you shall never again be allowed entry to the Otherworld."

"You shall also be stripped of your name. It is the name of a goddess and you, you are no longer our kin," said Selena, "you shall henceforth be known only as Nameless…"

"Oh no, sister," hissed Tsira, "they shall call me the Nameless Goddess, and I shall sing to them with nightmares that drive their fears and fuel their hatred…one day I will call forth an army the likes of which you have never imagined and I shall use them to crush you all."

"Until then…" said Nerwyn, god of the deep waters, stepping forth to touch Tsira upon the forehead. Tsira was cocooned in a sphere of dark blue light that transported her away from the Palace of the Dead, across the River Lethe, through the mists between the worlds, and into Albion. She was hurtled into the depths of a dark well on an island at the heart of the Marshland Forest, doomed to remain there indefinitely, the black water of the well becoming her flesh and chilling her fiery spirit with its frigid touch.

The Temple of the One God continued to thrive in the east but remained a small minority in the Atland for centuries to come. The Tetrarchs never suspected their One God had been murdered by the Nameless Goddess. They created an elaborate story about how the One God had ascended into the heavens to create a palace amidst the stars where the faithful would one day join him after taking their last breath. The gods and goddesses did nothing to dissuade the followers of the One God for without the presence of Theis, their prayers were not fueling the power of a deity. They were simply worshipping an idol that had long since passed away from the living world.

The gods and goddesses were not content with allowing mankind to implode into a sea of violence and hatred. They sent forth a call into the universe, bringing Elfkind to the shores of the Atland from their own home amidst the stars, to guide men towards a religion that would maintain the worship of the Old Gods through the pursuit of peace, compassion, and untainted wisdom…

Cyndriel and Norvo

Norvo was raised in the wilds of Lemuria, born in the first days after the Old Gods departed from the living world. His tribe lived nomadically, traveling across the grasslands bordering the great Brytewood Forest in the northern highlands of Lemuria. Norvo was an Easterling, accustomed to the newly established authority of the Temple of the One God in the Sun Pyramid, once serving as home to the Old Gods. He spent his days fishing and gathering fruit from the tapari trees. He often ventured off on his own to explore the overgrown groves of Brytewood, where the tapari trees grew especially tall, and there amongst the brambles he discovered an old, decaying ring of knee-high stones surrounding a large flat altar. Thinking the altar the perfect place to take a quick afternoon nap, Norvo laid down on the smooth stone and went to sleep. He had a strange dream where he was enveloped in cold, silver mists and carried away to another world.

When Norvo woke, he was still lying on the altar in the fairy ring but the Brytewood had vanished. In its place was a sprawling grassland filled with wild flowers and apple trees. In the distance, a wide river flowed swiftly towards the horizon and behind him stood high snow-capped mountains. Norvo panicked. He thought he was still sleeping and began to pinch himself on the arm, desperate to wake up in the comfortable and familiar Brytewood, near his family and home. But he wasn't asleep. As chance would have it, while he dreamed within the fairy ring, he quietly slipped from the living world and into Avalon, the place between places guarding the crossing to the Otherworld. Norvo was aware of the mythical land of the faeries but he didn't believe it truly existed. It was a story parents told their children to get them to sleep. Fantastic tales of the men beyond the mists who weren't really men at all. They were shapeshifters, able to take on any form or face they chose or be completely unseen, living as one with the elements in the wilds of the natural world. They were possessed of a magic that put the power of the Art to shame and were, as the stories said, the first occupants of the living world.

Norvo walked towards the snowcapped mountains for nearly an hour. Eventually he came over a small ridge and was greeted by a beautiful city filled with buildings of crimson, magenta, and shades of yellow. Before he could come any closer, a gorgeous young man appeared a few feet from Norvo. His fiery red hair was so long it touched the top of his buttocks as it waved wildly like it was a sail filled by a strong zephyr. He was naked and his athletic body shimmered, as though he had recently bathed in olive oil. Norvo was himself a rare beauty, with skin the color of sand and shiny hair as black as coal, but his good looks paled in comparison to the intoxicating allure of the man standing in front of him, seemingly sculpted by the hands of the Old Gods themselves.

"You're not a fairy," said the faerie-man after sniffing the air.

"I should say not," replied Norvo.

"What are you?" said the faerie-man, ""I've never smelled anything like you before…"

"I'm a man."

"I've never heard of such a thing. Are you from near here?"

"I don't think so," replied Norvo, "I'm beginning to think my home is very far away."

The naked faerie-man looked at Norvo quizzically, like he didn't understand his answer before two butterfly wings materialized on his back and he took flight, circling Norvo playfully, like a cat ready to pounce on its favorite toy.

"Well, whatever you are, you smell really good," said the faerie-man, "You want to play with me?"

Norvo was overcome by a warm sensation that urged him to strip off his clothes and run after the faerie-man across the wide fields at the foothills of the snow-capped mountains. The faerie-man, a princeling named Cyndriel, led Norvo towards the distant river, to a fort made from clovers. They dipped their feet in the water then ran after each other, wrestling jovially in the patches of wild flowers growing on the shores of the river. Norvo ran his hands across Cyndriel's body, feeling the taut curves of his muscles and the firmness in his loins. Cyndriel allowed Norvo to explore the contours and crevices of his body without objection, lying motionless in the grass with a subtle smile of satisfaction. Norvo kissed Cyndriel on his lips and his nose and his ears. He ran his tongue down the line running the length of Cyndriel's back and tickled his genitalia with his nose. Norvo hadn't felt sexual urges for another man before but, as he embraced Cyndriel, he knew he'd one day fall in love with him, that the exotic faerie princeling would be his greatest joy and his ultimate undoing. Norvo fell on top of Cyndriel, sliding his manhood into the narrow ravine of his buttocks. Cyndriel uttered not one sound as Norvo drove his member deeper and deeper, harder and harder, exploding in ephemeral waves of orgasm, momentarily sapping him of his vitality and strength.

"I didn't hurt you, did I?" asked Norvo, falling onto the grass and wrapping his arms around Cyndriel.

"No," said Cyndriel with the voice of an automaton before leaping up and bounding off towards the river. He jumped as he reached the shore and, before he hit the water, he had transformed into a fish.

Norvo was sure Cyndriel had abandoned him. He would've dressed if he had kept track of his clothes and then run off in shame. But to his surprise, only minutes after Cyndriel had transformed into a fish and swam away, he reappeared above Norvo, shifting from a small hummingbird into his human-looking self. He ran back to Norvo and threw him to the ground, jumping on top of him and pushing Norvo eagerly back into him. They made love three more times before Cyndriel was at last exhausted. As the sun began to set and the gray moon rose into the sky, Cyndriel and Norvo sat lazily on the edge of the silver water, intertwined in each other's arms.

"What else can you turn into?" asked Norvo, "besides a fish and a hummingbird."

"And this form," added Cyndriel.

"You don't really look like this?" said Norvo.

"I don't really look like anything."

"I'm not sure I understand."

"You won't," said Cyndriel, "my true form is beyond your comprehension. But you were wondering about what I can become…"

Cyndriel stood and sauntered a few feet away from Norvo. With a slight tremor of his flesh, Cyndriel shrank into a mouse with brown fur and a long tail. He sprang roots and became a primrose with petals as pink as the belly of a salmon. The flower then became a tall oak tree, then a tower of stone before shrinking into a common housecat that traipsed over to Norvo and jumped into his lap. As Norvo stroked the tabby's mane it shifted back into the man with whom Norvo was falling in love.

"That was amazing," said Norvo sleepily.

"You should rest," said Cyndriel, "I'll keep you warm."

Norvo expected Cyndriel to pull him into his chest and allow his body heat to blanket Norvo but Cyndriel stood and, with a little hop, transformed into a small campfire complete with a hearth of stones. Norvo laid down near the hearth and fell into a deep sleep.

Norvo awoke to the sound of a woman's voice.

"I can't believe this," she said.

He opened his eyes to see a tall and immensely attractive naked woman, nearly identical to Cyndriel, standing over him. Norvo thought she was speaking to him until he realized she was looking at the fire still burning lazily in the circle of stones. The fire sputtered out as the human Cyndriel took shape in front of the woman, his arms crossed, his eyes narrow, and his brow furrowed.

"You can't believe what, mother?" snapped Cyndriel.

"I can't believe I would find you here cavorting with this animal when you should be at my side," said the woman angrily.

"Excuse me," interjected Norvo defensively, "but I'm no animal."

"Be silent, filthy beast," replied the woman, "I am Queen. You would do well to remember your place…"

The faerie queen grabbed her son by the ear and, the second her fingers made contact with his skin, he was absorbed into her, like a drop of rain joining the ocean. Her eyes flickered with a spark of orange fire before she turned to stare down at Norvo. She grew in stature and presence, blocking out the light of the morning sun and casting a terrifying shadow across him.

"I do not know how you came to be in my kingdom, man-beast, nor do I care…all that concerns me is you find your way back to where you came from quickly," she said coldly before transforming into a raven and flying away towards the city in the distance.

Norvo sat there, bewildered by the banks of the river. He didn't know how to get the fairy ring to take him home. He wasn't sure where he was and he had no idea the way to free himself from the deep urges within his mind, driving him to think only of Cyndriel. He reluctantly decided he had just one choice: he would have to enter the city of the faeries and track down his true love. He was concerned about his scent, a seemingly tell-tale sign of his humanity, so he rubbed himself in mud and found some squirrel scat to carry in his pocket before setting out for the wondrous city on the horizon.

Nephanduil, the City of the Stars, was a non-walled metropolis stretching out across the grasslands at the foot of the snow-capped mountains of Avalon. The city was unguarded and didn't possess any weapons or natural defenses. The faeries were the only sentient beings living in Avalon and were a peaceful people without war or disease. Norvo entered the city quietly, without drawing attention, during the early hours of morning when, he hoped, the faeries would be in their beds. The city was silent as he wandered its narrow streets in search of Cyndriel.

He was unexplainably drawn to a tall crimson tower at the heart of the city, as though he were a piece of metal being pulled by a powerful magnet. He silently climbed the seemingly endless stairs until he came to a landing at the top, overlooking the city and the sprawling meadows beyond. On a pedestal near the edge of the terrace sat a small bronze urn with a glass window on its side. Norvo could see a strange green liquid sloshing within the urn, as though it was a miniature ocean being pulled and churned by the magnetism of the moon. Norvo passed by the pedestal on his way to a set of doors on the wall of the terrace when he heard the disincarnate voice of Cyndriel resonating from the depths of the urn.

"I'm in the jar my darling," said Cyndriel, *"Do not try to open it…any hand that touches the lid, be it man or be it fae, will be burned away as though it never existed. My mother has potent magic…I know of none with the power to break this charm."*

"There has to be a way," said Norvo out loud.

"I can only think of one. Have you ever heard of a Callim Lamp?"

"No."

"It's a rare artifact with the power to trap a faerie inside it…my mother has one in the cabinet behind her bed. If you were to steal it and light it in her presence, she would be drawn inside. Even her magic isn't strong enough to resist the Callim…"

"How can I possibly steal a lamp from a cabinet behind your mother's bed?" said Norvo, "I'm guessing it won't be while she's in it."

"She's never in it and she won't be expecting you to try something so bold. I think it might work."

"I don't know."

"Trust me, Norvo. We have to try."

Norvo was willing to do anything to reunite with his lover and went warily back into the tower, moving slowly towards the lower levels where the queen's private rooms were situated. The queen wasn't present in her chambers and Norvo immediately located the cabinet containing the Callim Lamp, a strange looking lantern crafted from stone, but the cabinet door was locked. He panicked until he saw a shiny key hanging from a ribbon on the wall by the door. It fit perfectly into the lock and, with a click, Norvo slid the door open and retrieved the lamp.

"It's very beautiful, isn't it?" said the queen, appearing behind Norvo in the archway near her bed.

Norvo backed up against the wall beneath a torch as the queen advanced towards him. Her menacing smile faded as she read the signs on Norvo's face, the lines of guilt confessing his intentions. She ran one of her cold fingers along Norvo's cheek and he shivered at her eerie touch.

"You're quite attractive for a mongrel," she said, "if circumstances were different I might keep you as a pet."

"You're an awful woman," replied Norvo.

"I'm no woman."

The faerie queen transformed into a massive serpent with eyes like a cat, the fangs of a viper, and a giant tail filling the room. She bore down on Norvo, snapping at his head with her enormous mouth, but he avoided her by tucking himself under her nightstand. He was ousted by a sharp flick of her tail that sent him hurtling through the air into the wall, knocking the wind from his lungs and causing him to release his grip on the Callim Lamp. The lamp rolled across the floor, coming to rest against the serpent's slimy scales. It blinked its red eyes at Norvo before resuming its shape as the faerie queen who picked up the lamp and cradled it in her arms. She was terrifyingly beautiful but also intimidating and cold, like a jaded woman filled with a hatred for the world around her, seeking to strike out in malice because of fears long festering in the depths of her heart.

"Silly little man," she sneered, "you slipped through a portal into my world and thought you could steal my only son by using this lamp against me…I must applaud your bravery. I didn't think men could be moved to action by anything but greed and fear."

"You misjudge us, my lady."

"Perhaps…"

The faerie queen made her hand transform into the blade of a longsword and advanced on Norvo. He pulled himself off the floor and turned towards the wall, hoping he would find an exit that wasn't there before. He saw only the torch. Then it dawned on him. He yanked the torch down from the wall and tossed it at the faerie queen. She seemed not to realize the significance of what he had done. As the torch made contact with the lamp, which erupted into life, it cast a blazing purple glow over the room. The sycophantic smile melted from the faerie queen's face as she transformed into an owl and flew off towards the nearby window. She wasn't fast enough. The purple light acted like a net, wrapping the queen in its brilliance and pulling her reluctantly towards the lamp. The queen rapidly transformed from a rat to a bee, from a gust of wind to an eagle, before she melted into a puddle of green ooze surrounding a strange looking triangular white stone marked with luminescent symbols glowing with the same purple hue as the lamp. With a final burst of radiance, the lamp sucked the ooze and the stone inside its depths.

Norvo had no time to celebrate his victory. The moment the faerie queen vanished into the Callim Lamp the world around Norvo began to unravel. The walls of the tower slowly faded, stone by stone, the queen's bed vanished, and the doors were rendered intangible. The sky went black, like someone had turned out the stars and the river in the distance churned like it was being boiled. Norvo ran as fast as his legs would carry him to the top of the tower, to the urn containing the gelatinous Cyndriel.

"What's happening," he yelled.

"I don't know," replied Cyndriel weakly, *"what happened when you used the lamp on my mother?"*

"It sucked her inside it. It turned her into a pool of green goo and a weird white stone and then it sucked her up like a cistern collecting water."

"You say she turned into ooze and a white stone…was the stone triangular? Did it have glowing runes written on it?"

"Yes, why?" asked Norvo.

"My mother had the Summerstone…I didn't think it really existed but it does and it changes everything. You have to set her free, Norvo. You have to let my mother out so she can use the stone and stop this madness…"

The urn and the pedestal faded from existence before Cyndriel could finish, leaving Norvo alone on the rapidly disintegrating terrace. He ran towards the nearby stairs but they were gone. He turned towards the rear passage but it had disappeared. He began to think he wouldn't find a way to escape the tower before it came crashing down around him but, to his surprise, he blinked and found himself standing in the middle of a field at the base of the mountains. The tower and the City of the Stars were gone. Norvo raced towards the fairy ring that had carried him to Avalon but he couldn't find it. There were no traces of the faerie civilization, like they had never existed. Norvo studied the Callim Lamp, looking for an incantation or a locking mechanism to reverse its power and set the faerie queen free but, despite his rigorous efforts, the lamp would not give up its prisoner.

Norvo wandered through the untamed wilds of Avalon for days, the lamp held firmly in his fist, searching for a clue to setting things right and restoring the faeries. He was enamored by Cyndriel's beauty and charm but he wasn't willing to sacrifice the rest of the faerie population because of his irreverent stupidity.

On the seventh day of his wandering, Norvo came across a strange stone monolith standing near a hedge maze. It was shaped like a large wand pointing up at the heavens. The same runes adorning the Summerstone were

etched into its sides, also lit by a purple glow. Norvo traced the lines of the
runes with his fingers as his face was twisted by sadness. He sobbed softly,
remembering his lover and wishing for his home. The monolith vibrated
slightly and the runes grew brighter before a ghostly apparition materialized
in front of Norvo. It was Cyndriel but he was not really there. He was a
shadowy echo of the brilliant faerie he had been days before.

"Cyndriel?" asked Norvo in amazement, "Is that you?"

"I am but a copy of the creature you call Cyndriel," said the apparition, *"Sent
here from another reality with a message. Without the Summerstone, the faeries cannot
hope to manifest in this world. The stone is the conduit from which they are nurtured and
sustained. Without it, they are lost. You must find a way to free the queen and the stone,
or else we shall all be consigned forever to the vaults of nonbeing."*

"I'm not a wizard, or a priest," said Norvo, "I don't know how to
open the lamp. I've tried everything…nothing works."

*"You must find a way…but if the task proves too much for you and your days
grow long and weary drink from the river. Its waters will make you forget your past so you
may start anew, though the river cannot carry you back to your world. That door is shut…"*

The apparition vanished with those final haunting words. Norvo was
left to roam Avalon in search of food and shelter. He made his home on the
edge of a brackish lake in the foothills of the snow-capped mountains. He
fished in the streams and hunted the wild hares living in the nearby grasslands.
He allowed his beard and hair to grow into long, matted dreadlocks and
eventually lost most his teeth. A single year turned to two and then ten before
Norvo returned to the monolith with the Callim Lamp in his hands. His skin
had been darkened to a rich brown by the Avalon sun and streaks of white
were springing up in his hair. His eyes were yellowed and his few remaining
teeth were as brown as molasses.

"I'm sorry, Cyndriel," he said, "I'm not strong enough."

Norvo placed the lamp on the ground and touched the monolith
gently, like he was bidding farewell to a dying parent. There were no ghostly

apparitions or great flashes of light this time, only the gentle whisper of the wind as it blew through the reeds and wildflowers. Heavy with sadness, Norvo journeyed to the banks of the river. He jumped headfirst into the water, allowing it to fill his mouth and rush down his throat. He felt a calm surrender as his mind was washed clean. He forgot about Lemuria and his parents, about the faerie queen and the Callim Lamp. He couldn't remember his name or why he was floating in the river. Most importantly, he had no recollection of his lost lover.

The stories say Norvo still wanders the wild places of Avalon, a mad and eccentric ghost, searching in vain for his memories lost to the waters of the River Lethe...

Anaximander

Anaximander Anfa was born into the lowly serf caste during the reign of the Last Elfin Empress. As a serf, he was relegated to live an abysmal life as a simple farmhand with no power over his life or freedom to choose his destiny. Anaximander was a deeply unhappy child. He asked his mother and father why he couldn't become a priest or a politician, to which they always answered: "Because you weren't born a priest or a politician…you were born the son of a serf and a serf you will become." Anaximander felt obligated to respect his parents and asked no more questions. Secretly he decided one day he would journey to the Eternal City and ask the Last Elfin Empress why he couldn't become a priest or a politician. Surely the greatest of all Elfkind would know why men were born into castes and robbed of the chance to control their own futures.

The opportunity to find an answer to his questions came when Anaximander reached the age of manhood and was sold to the Lord Rannok. He was put to work in his new master's gardens at the heart of the Eternal City, only yards from the Palace of Silver Light and the Last Elfin Empress. For months he schemed about gaining access to her heavenly person. He resolved to borrow some of Lord Rannok's robes and disguise himself as a highborn. He took care to comb his hair properly and to trim his beard. He washed in the stream near the edge of the gardens and stole a bottle of scent from the master's laundress before setting out towards the palace.

Anaximander was relieved when no one looked in his direction as he entered the Palace of Silver Light by way of its grand public entrance. It was half passed noon, when the Last Elfin Empress would be holding audiences in the throne room. Anaximander hurried along the corridors in the direction he hoped would lead him there. The palace was extraordinarily large, much bigger than it appeared on the outside, with halls filled by marble columns and torches burning with green flames. He stumbled into the throne room by accident and was astounded by what he saw before him. Upon a large white marble throne, etched into the likeness of a tree, sat an otherworldly creature that vaguely resembled a human. Its skin was as white as milk and its face was lacking a nose and lips. It bore only a slit for a mouth and two bulbous eyes the color of molten silver, staring down at Anaximander without blinking. Its hair was like dried twigs fallen from an old growth tree and it had long pointed ears with fur growing from the inner lobes. The only thing that distinguished it as female was the long white gown of silk it wore to conceal its strangely shaped breasts and elongated limbs.

"*You are not what you seem, my Lord,*" said a majestic female voice within Anaximander's mind, "*Why have you come to hold an audience with us this day? Is it the question that even now aches to be answered, buried in the deep places of your soul?*"

"How did you know?" asked Anaximander.

The Last Elfin Empress' stare burned into Anaximander and he felt himself compelled to tell her the truth.

"I am a lowborn serf," he confessed.

"*I know. I can see the things that men try to hide as though they are wearing their secrets painted upon their foreheads,*" laughed the empress from inside of Anaximander's head.

"Then you should know the nature of my question...why must there be castes in Albion? Shouldn't men be free to pursue their own dreams with the liberty to make their own choices...isn't choice central to the laws of the Old Religion?"

"*Not all choices can be made by a man. Men do not always understand the Deep Mysteries of nature and must be led down the right path by those who are wiser.*"

"And who is it that decided this?"

"*It was by the will of the gods the castes of men were born.*"

"Then I wish to address the gods directly," said Anaximander bluntly. The other men in the room, who were servants of the Last Elfin Empress, laughed quietly under their breath.

"It cannot be done," said the empress, using her own voice for the first time, a deep languid voice which resonated throughout the room, "no mortal man may enter the world of the deep shadows mirroring our own…such is the law."

"Whose law?" asked Anaximander.

"You are a smart one, aren't you?" smiled the empress, "it is my law…but I tell you now, no living man has ever succeeded in crossing the River of the Dead. Before you can reach the shores of that distant river, you must pass the tests of the four sphinxes…something not many are capable of achieving."

"I think you underestimate me, majesty. If you show me where I might find these sphinxes I will be on my way."

"If only it were that simple. Tell me, son of Osinarmen, what do you know of the Art?"

"I know nothing of magic."

"The question was rhetorical, dear one. The point is that you must know the Deep Mysteries of the Art to find the path leading to the River Lethe. Have you never heard of the barrier that separates our world from that otherworld of the dead? Your people call it the Mists. It is a secret only the greatest wizards and priests know. Before you talk of reaching the sphinxes, you must first learn how to call the Mists. That, my child, will take you years, if not the whole of your natural life."

"I will find a way, majesty."

"*I admire your persistence, son of Osinarmen, and wish you all the best, though I do not believe you will succeed,*" said the empress telepathically.

Anaximander smiled as he left the palace and returned to the gardens that had become his home. He found a purpose that was greater than the bonds into which he had been born, a choice to either take the word of the Last Elfin Empress and give up, or abandon the law of the castes and begin learning the Art.

Finding someone willing to teach him the Art was impossible, given the strict laws of wizards and priests, preventing laypeople from studying the Deep Mysteries. Instead, he turned to ancient scrolls relegated to the vast basement storage of his master, Lord Rannok. The scrolls gave him enough knowledge to learn how to cast a sacred circle and call forth elemental guardians. He learned how to influence fire and wind through these elemental beings. He discovered how to project his consciousness over great distances, to observe events as a ghost living unseen in the shadows. He even figured out how to glamour himself so that, to the world around him, he appeared to be someone else entirely. But, try as he might, he did not discover the secret of calling the Mists. For years Anaximander poured over those old parchments before resolving he would leave behind the Eternal City and seek out a teacher in a foreign land. With his newly acquired powers, he was able to *convince* his master to grant him his freedom and used his *influence* to hire a boat captain to take him abroad.

He found what his heart desired in Lemuria, within the remains of the Pyramid of the Sun. In the dark and abandoned libraries of those distant ruins, he found the spell to summon the mists.

"Ena imarawe atar," he said loudly, his eyes clenched shut.

When Anaximander opened his eyes again, the world around him had given way to a thick curtain of gray fog through which Anaximander could not see. Every direction he looked, the mists shrouded the outside world. He felt a deep chill penetrating his bones, causing him to shake with a sharp pain threatening to bring him to his knees. He doubled over from the unbearable aching in his stomach and sides, summoning just enough strength to speak the second half of the spell.

"Rora karenthir atman," he sputtered.

He was dizzy and nauseous as the mists parted like a curtain on a stage, revealing a meadow of bluegrass and wild flowers blooming in droves with wild hares bounding freely towards a river flowing swiftly in the distance. Anaximander crawled down the narrow aisle between the mists and found himself lying on the grass beneath the warmth of a clear morning sun. He breathed deeply as his strength slowly returned. As he stood the mists dissolved, exposing the rest of the prairie running off towards a range of snowcapped mountains. There were no traces of civilization, no crumbling foundations, no old buildings leaning from neglect, no broken windows, no rotting doors. Only untouched nature, as though no living hand had ever touched it. Anaximander thought about resting awhile amidst a cluster of daisies but decided he'd better push on towards the river.

As he came nearer to the water, Anaximander noticed a wide ravine barring his way. He followed the ravine to its edge and was greeted by a tall and intimidating hedge maze. The light of the sun was dampened by an invisible shadow as Anaximander entered. He was confident he could face whatever challenges awaited him. He had gone no further than a mile when he was greeted by a giant sphinx with bright red eyes, standing beside a tall silver mirror.

"I am the guardian of truth," said the sphinx, "look into the mirror and tell me what you see."

"I see a man," said Anaximander, "nothing more, nothing less."

"Very good," replied the sphinx, "no man may pass my gate who believes himself greater than his peers…all men are equal before the gods."

The glass of the mirror dissolved, exposing an archway leading into the next section of the maze. Anaximander continued with care, making sure to judge carefully every path he chose. Within minutes, he came to another dead-end where a second giant sphinx was standing next to a large door.

"I am the guardian of wisdom," said the sphinx, "step through the door and demonstrate the virility of your mind."

As he opened the door and stepped through to the other side, Anaximander was greeted by a large mob of people chasing a woman down the narrow alley of an unknown city. Anaximander ran after them, coming to a small courtyard where the woman had been backed into a corner. He sprinted to intercept the mob, standing between the woman and her pursuers in the hopes he might prevent them from bringing her harm.

"What is the meaning of this?" shouted Anaximander.

"It is none of your business," replied a fat man.

"I'm making it my business," said Anaximander.

"This woman is a criminal," sneered an elderly woman.

"She deserves to die for her crimes," sneered the fat man.

"Yes," echoed the mob in unison, "death!"

"What crime has she committed?" demanded Anaximander.

"She stole food from my market," yelled the fat man.

"Why would you steal from this man?" Anaximander asked the frightened woman.

"Because, sir," she said meekly, "my children are starving and I haven't the means to feed them."

"That's not the worst of it," shouted the elderly woman, "she murdered my son in cold blood..."

"Your son was a brute," said the woman, "he tried to rape me."

"What about my daughter," said a young man, "Did she deserve to be beat by you?"

"Your daughter was attacking mine," said the woman, "I could think of nothing else but to give your wretched child the spanking she's long deserved."

"We don't care what you say," shouted multiple people, "you are a criminal...you deserve to die."

"I don't think so," said Anaximander, "this woman may be guilty of these crimes, and she may not, but it is not for any of us to decide. She must be brought to trial fairly in a court of law so that proper magistrates may judge her without bias."

"We don't have to listen to you," barked the fat man, "we'll just take her and string her up by the nearest tree."

"I will face any man who tries," said Anaximander, "and I warn you now, I have spent many years studying the Art. Do you think your weapons will keep you safe from the magic I wield?"

"Very good," said the accused woman. The mob vanished as the woman transformed into the sphinx.

"It takes great wisdom to recognize the difference between justice and revenge," said the sphinx, "you may pass..."

The same door which had led Anaximander to the mob appeared on the wall, allowing him to pass into the next section of the maze and continue his journey where he came to a third sphinx standing next to a well so deep Anaximander couldn't see the bottom. The sphinx turned to Anaximander and spoke with a deep, resonant voice.

"I am the guardian of courage," it said, "and my test is simple...if you wish to pass, you must jump into the well..."

Anaximander stared into the depths of the vertical shaft. He saw no trace of water, only darkness descending in an endless freefall. The likelihood of any mortal surviving such a leap was extremely slim. But Anaximander had come this far and was not about to turn back. With a deep breath, he closed his eyes and started to leap. His feet had yet to leave the ground when the sphinx spoke again.

"Stop," it said, "you need not jump. Your willingness to do so illustrates your strength and determination. You may continue..."

A tunnel appeared where the deep cavernous well had been, leading Anaximander into the final section of the maze. He immediately encountered the fourth sphinx who was much larger than her sisters. This sphinx was standing on the edge of the River of the Dead and Anaximander saw the distant shores of the Otherworld, stretching out forever towards the horizon, lush and green and full of life without the living.

"You have come to the banks of the River Lethe to face your final challenge. Unlike my sisters, I am no guardian…I am a judge meant to recall for you the worst moments of your life, to bring them into the forefront of your mind, that you may experience them again. Only then will we know if you are indeed pure enough to cross into the realm of our gods."

Anaximander was wrapped in darkness, as though the sun had been a candle blown out by a strong wind. Then a scene materialized before him of a little boy sitting at a roughhewn dining table at the heart of a thatch-roof hut. The boy was crying while a stern unfeeling woman towered over him, a horse crop held tightly in her fist.

"When will you learn your place, Anax?" said the woman, "you are nothing more than a worthless serf…you could die tomorrow and it would make little difference to the world around us. The quicker you learn that, the better off you'll be. I'm going to beat you with this crop and, with each lash, I want you to tell me you are only a lowly serf."

The beating was fierce, with more than fifty lashes inflicted on the young Anaximander's back and legs. With each swipe of the belt, he did as his mother asked and whimpered.

"I am only a lowly serf."

The little Anaximander and his mother faded into the shadows as another Anaximander took their place. This one was an adolescent with a cracking voice and hair springing up in strange places. He was running along a field with one of the other serf-children, having finished his daily chores early and desiring a bath in the warm waters of the nearby pond.

"What do you want to be when you grow up?" Anaximander asked the other little boy while they swam lazily.

The little boy looked at Anaximander with his brow furrowed, as though he had not understood the question.

"I'll be a farmhand, same as you," said the boy.

"I'm not going to be a farmhand," said Anaximander, "I'm going to study the Art and join the Wyt Robes."

"You can't," replied the boy, "you weren't born in the wizarding clans."

"I'm going to be the greatest Wyt Robe the world has ever seen."

That night the little boy went home and told his mother about Anaximander's story. The next day she visited Anaximander's mother, insisting she beat him for spinning such lies. It didn't take much to convince Anaximander's mother. She took the horse crop to him and again he was whipped. This Anaximander faded into the shadows and, for a third time, another one appeared. This one was a young adult. He was kneeling on his knees before a harsh looking old man wearing green velvet robes and holding a whip in his left hand.

"You should be killed for such insolence," said the man with the whip, "I have half a mind to string you up at the gates."

"I'm sorry, m'Lord Rannok," said the young Anaximander, "but I'm not happy here. I wish to learn and to grow…what man wouldn't."

"A man who know his place," snapped Rannok, "a serf doesn't have the right to visit the empress…the fact that you even looked upon her face is treason. If I didn't like you as much as I do, Anax, I would turn you over to the magistrates and allow justice to be done."

Everything went dark and the voice of the sphinx began echoing in the endless nothingness like thunder shaking high mountain passes during a powerful winter storm.

"Tell me, Anaximander, son of Osinarmen, son of Uleya, if you had the power to do so, would you wish harm upon those who have wronged you? Would you like to teach Lord Rannok a lesson or take a riding crop to your hateful mother's hide? I can see the deep places of your mind. I know the pain you have endured…don't you want vengeance?"

"I do not," said Anaximander, "I don't need revenge. The nature of our choices delivers to us the blessings or hardships we deserve. My mother died alone and in immense pain and Rannok eventually lost all his wealth and prestige. I didn't need to seek revenge. The universe sought it out for me."

Anaximander regained his senses and was again standing on the banks of the River Lethe. The large sphinx, who had been joined by her three sisters, held out one of her massive fists. She opened it to reveal two small gold coins marked with the elfin crest.

"You must pay the ferryman for safe passage," said the sphinx, "one coin for your departure, one for your return…be well, son of Osinarmen, you have a great destiny awaiting you."

"Many thanks," said Anaximander.

Down a narrow path behind the sphinxes sat an old crumbling dock with a small barge tied to it. Anaximander thought he would have to guide himself across the waters until a skeletal man wrapped in a dirty brown cloak stepped out from behind a tree, his yellowed, blind eyes staring vacantly in Anaximander's direction.

"Payment," he hissed, holding out his decrepit, rotting hand to receive one of the two gold coins. The ferryman grabbed a long pole made from petrified wood. He stood at the back of the barge while Anaximander took a seat near the front. The water didn't seem to be disturbed by the pole, neither rippling nor distorting its surface. It remained like a sheet of glass reflecting the light of the setting sun like a mirror. As Anaximander crossed the center of the river, he felt a great chill enter his bones, like the one that assaulted him after calling the mists, but the sensation was fleeting and was followed by a comforting warm breeze.

The rest of the story is unknown to man. Anaximander was gone from the living world for hundreds of years. When he returned, he was so changed that, if any who had known him in his youth were to look upon him, they would not recognize him in any way. It is believed Anaximander indeed reached the Palace of the Dead, beyond the Fields of the Ever-Living, in that Otherworld we all go to when we die. His time there blessed him with near-everlasting life and a power over magic possessed by very few. He came to be called the Wandering Wizard because he took no mortal home, always following the distant horizon in search of hidden treasures lost to the passing of time. To the few he called his friends, he may have revealed the secrets of his experiences across the River Lethe but, with the rest of us, he never shared anything.

Shortly after his return to the living world, Anaximander was given an audience with the first Wyt King, the usurper of the crown of Atlantis responsible for the disappearance of Elfkind. He was brought to the very throne room where he met the Last Elfin Empress hundreds of years before. The Tree-Throne had been torn down and replaced by a squared throne of black rock bearing the Yellow Rose of the One God. Anaximander recounted all his wondrous adventures for the Wyt King, except those secret days spent amongst the Old Gods in the Otherworld. After the great labor of recounting his tales, the Wyt King was thoroughly satisfied.

"Tell me, wizard," said the Wyt King, "Did you ever discover why the Old Gods forced their caste systems on man?"

Anaximander smiled warmly.

"I did, your Grace," said Anaximander, "but I'm afraid you wouldn't like the answer."

No More Elfkind

Most the men of the Atland have forgotten the Eternal City was not built by the hand of man but by the awesome powers of Elfkind. The golden walls were raised by the first High King. The river avenues and palatial buildings were raised and filled by the First Elfin Empress. The entire city sprang up overnight, shining from the heart of the Atland like a beacon guiding pilgrims towards the gates of heaven. Elfkind descended from the stars at the dawn of time to bring peace and order to the living world and forge the great kingdom of Albion. Elfkind was at first welcomed by men, except by those few followers of the Temple of the One God who viewed the Old Gods of Elfkind to be idolatrous and evil, retreating to Lemuria in fear and did not come again to the Atland for many centuries.

The men who remained in the Atland under the tutelage of Elfkind grew in both wisdom and prosperity, always endeavoring to maintain peace amongst their tribes. They erected hundreds of temples honoring the Old Gods and held the High Sabbats as the most sacred days of the year. They began learning the light in the Art from their elfin masters, as well as language, swordsmithing, gemcrafting, government, and music. Dozens of small cities were built in the likeness of Atlantis throughout Albion. Suddenly the whole world was under the rule of the Elfin Empress, except the islands of Lemuria and the Xani Highlands in the northeast. The Old Nobility and Wizarding Clans were created from the ranks of the faithful by the Elfin Empresses who came in due succession to sit upon the throne. The nobility became responsible for the administration of the small lands and cities in the name of the Old Gods through the promotion of peace. Elfkind had no rivals with the strength to oppose them as they cemented the ancestral culture and traditions of the Atlandish peoples. War ceased in Albion as the banners of the Elfin Empresses and their High Kings were raised above the noble houses across Albion.

Unfortunately not all was completely peaceful beneath the surface as Elfkind bickered amongst themselves for supremacy. They came to Albion to promote peace in the name of the Old Gods but failed to see the power of the darkness lurking in the shadows. The powerful Amulet of the One God fell into the hands of a fallen god who decided to make a bid for absolute supremacy and descended into the living world with a power never before seen by the eyes of mortals. His name from the dawn of time had been Ragnar, god of twilight, but that name was stripped from him by the other gods when he fell into darkness. From then on he was called the Black Prince, a fearsome necromancer with the power to steal the souls of men and use them to raise the dead from their graves. Almost all Elfkind, including the Elfin Empress Saavika III, stood against the Black Prince but many were led by the High King Valan Longbow, joining forces with the fallen god and his powerful amulet. Men were also divided. The Old Nobility stood behind their Empress while the peasantry joined with the enemy after he promised to abolish the caste system imposed on man by Elfkind, inciting a great rebellion amidst the discontented men of the Atland.

Albion was plunged into a civil war, devastating the environment and bringing pestilence and famine to men for the first time in recorded history. Many men turned to the Black Prince simply because he made promises to feed them and provide them with gold, promises that went forever unfulfilled. The Elfin Empress and her followers did what they could to protect the Atland and keep out the evil threatening them from abroad but she underestimated the power of the Amulet of the One God. The Black Prince used it to crush their defenses in one afternoon, bringing war to the heart of Albion. The river avenues were filled with the blood of the innocent and the temples of the Old Gods were pulled down from their foundations and burned to ashes. The living world was brought to the brink of ruin as men became discontented with their fate on both sides of the war.

The war raged for three centuries, with the population of Albion brought to its lowest point since man crawled forth from their caves at the dawn of time. Saavika III sacrificed herself and bound her soul to the talisman called the Autumn Crown, hoping to level the playing field and provide her daughter the opportunity to defeat the Black Prince.

Xanyra, daughter of Saavika III, walked defiantly into the heart of the Black Prince's dominion, striking down all who faced her with the power of her crown, until she came upon the Black Prince himself. Their battle was one of legend. The light of their magic could be seen from the Eternal City and all the foul architecture built in the darkness was torn down by the brilliance of Xanyra's light. Finally Xanyra succeeded in ripping the Black Prince's amulet from his hands, transforming him into a withered old gnomish-man as punishment for his crimes. She took the Amulet of the One God into her possession and passed the Autumn Crown to her daughter, Eanora. Eanora became the Last Elfin Empress and began restoring order to a world ravaged by darkness. Meanwhile, Xanyra built for herself a mighty red tower on the edge of the Wynterlande Forest. There she watched the passing of time through her enchanted mirrors, waiting for the day when the Black Prince might again try to bring his evil to the shores of Albion.

The Last Elfin Empress tried to restore peace to the living world but men had lost their faith in the power of Elfkind. They were unwilling to return to their rigid caste systems and denied the rights of Elfkind to act as their superiors. The opposition to the Last Elfin Empress was led by a Wyt Robe of great renown named Theron Kalenti.

"We cannot allow the elfin lords to return to their seats of power," said Theron to a crowd of men at the heart of the Eternal City.

"What can we do?" yelled someone from the crowd, "the Empress has her enchanted crown to protect her. What do we have? A few old spellbooks and a bunch of wizards too busy arguing amongst themselves to give a damn about us."

"We must rely on the power of our spirits," replied Theron.

"Our spirits are broken," said a young woman.

"Then we must find a way to mend them," said Theron, "I promise you we will find a way to free ourselves from the tyranny of the Empress and all her wretched kin."

Theron held true to his word, setting out to raise a massive army to oppose the Last Elfin Empress. He went to Lemuria to recruit the followers of the Temple of the One God, who were more than willing to bring war against Elfkind in the name of their religion. He then went north to Frozenland near the Wynterlande Forest and brought the Norn Giants into his service. He already had the majority of Atlandish men under his banners but still felt his army was not formidable enough to face the last remnants of the undefeated Elfin Knights. In the tradition of the Wyt Robes, Theron poured his soul into a talisman to hone and enhance his magic. Unlike other wizards, he gathered the souls of the warriors who fell under his banners and added them to his ring. In only a year, his ring grew powerful enough to rival the godly talismans. He was finally ready to make his war against Elfkind.

In a single day the armies of Theron succeeded in penetrating the walls of the Eternal City but were met by the full host of the Elfin Knights who drove them back into the sea. Theron crept into the city under the cover of darkness, wrapping himself in the shadows, walking unseen by the eyes of others. He entered the Palace of Silver Light by way of the western stairs and secretly came to the great hall. The Last Elfin Empress was seated upon her throne with the Autumn Crown perched on her head, watching the battle unfold on the streets below through the glass of an enchanted mirror held in her hands.

"I have been waiting for you," she said.

"Then you know why I have come," replied Theron.

"You think I am to blame for all the hardships men still endure," she said, "but you fail to understand the enormity of the devastation done to Albion by the Black Prince…the Atland has slowly begun to sink beneath the waves of the violent sea. It is taking all the power that we here possess to reverse the process. If we are no longer here then the Atland will one day be destroyed forever. Would you really bring ruin to all that we have built just to be rid of me and my people?"

"I would do anything to ensure the freedom of my people…"

"Spoken like a true king."

Theron moved as fast as his enchanted ring could carry him, appearing as nothing more than a blur moving towards the throne. The Last Elfin Empress used her crown to stop him dead in his tracks, lifting him off the ground and pulling him through the air to hover before her. Her bulbous silver eyes were filled with tears as she looked lovingly upon his face.

"I wish you could see the love we bear for you," said the Last Elfin Empress.

"I see only suppression," said Theron.

"I will not kill you, son of Aeron. I have seen too many fall needlessly in these wars…I yearn only for peace."

"As do I," said Theron, resisting the power of the empress long enough to reach out his hand and pluck the Autumn Crown from her head. He fell to the ground as the Last Elfin Empress cried out like she was enduring some indescribable pain.

"What have you done?" she yelled, clutching at her head with her long pointy fingers.

"I have freed my people," he said before placing the crown upon his head. With the power of his ring and the crown combined he was temporarily transmuted from a man into the apparition of a living god as he uttered a powerful magical command to the empress.

"No More Elfkind," he said with a thunderous voice.

In the blink of an eye the Last Elfin Empress disappeared, as though she had never been there, as did her guards and all the Elfin Knights securing the streets below. Everywhere, in every corner of Albion, Elfkind vanished without a trace. Only their glorious architecture remained as a reminder of their magnificent existence.

Three Elfkind survived because they were not present in the living world at the time, having journeyed through the mists to the Otherworld to entreat the Old Gods for aid. Upon their return, they found Albion forever changed and all their kind vanished. The Lady Rheis, eldest daughter of the Last Elfin Empress, decided to go to the Eternal City and investigate the disappearance. The other two Elfkind went their separate ways, one retreating into the Wynterlande Forest to take up the protection of the Amulet of the One God, known forever after as the Red Witch, and the other journeying into the east to settle in the Sylveroad Woods, yearning for nothing more than a simple life free of the violence that brought the world to the brink of destruction.

The Lady Rheis found the Palace of Silver Light filled with Atlandish men of every walk and every caste, rejoicing in celebration and homage beneath the flag of the Temple of the One God and white banners depicting a great eagle swooping down upon an unsuspecting badger. At the head of the crowd stood Theron Kalenti, dressed in the finest white robes embroidered with silver thread, wearing the Autumn Crown on his head and the Ring of a Hundred Souls upon his finger. He looked every bit the part of a monarch as he addressed the people standing before him with a regal voice that echoed through the great hall.

"At last the tyranny of the elves is gone," he said authoritatively, "we now stand upon the edge of a new era, one to be forged solely by the hands of man for the benefit of man…there shall be no more castes and no more conditions beyond the yearning of each individual soul. If you choose to worship the Old Gods or to congregate in the Temple of the One God, you shall be free to do so…you may practice the Art if you choose and how you see fit now and forever under the banners of liberty."

"Long live the Wyt King," cheered the crowd.

The Lady Rheis took advantage of the distraction to call the Autumn Crown from the king's head into her waiting hands. The Autumn Crown was forged by an elfin soul and yearned above all to be held in the hands of Elfkind. She placed it upon her head and invoked a spell that made her grow taller than a Norn Giant until she loomed over the crowd like a living tower. She meant to punish them all for the disappearance of her people and the demise of her mother but her temper was quickly checked as she spoke with a voice like an avalanche falling down a mountainside.

"I care not what you have done," she boomed, "but I warn you now…any ill-fate that has befallen my people will return to you nine fold, for such is the law of the Art…I will not make war upon you but neither will I live amidst your ranks. I will find a place beyond the sea where the old ways will remain strong and alive…any man of peaceful heart and compassionate will who wishes to live as we did before the wars will be welcome but none who seek to harm us will pass our borders."

The Lady Rheis vanished in a cloud of white smoke that loomed over the men below like a cloud threatening to rain. The men looked at one another in confusion before turning towards the Wyt King for answers.

"We shall not fear a lone elfin witch," said the Wyt King, "even with the Autumn Crown, she is no match for us…"

"But what if there are others?" said someone in the crowd.

"I promise you there are not," replied the king, "I will find an answer to why this she-elf survived and when I do I will discover a way to unmake her…until then we shall leave her to her own devices…we must now focus on rebuilding our kingdom."

The Wyt King did exactly as he promised. The caste systems were abolished forever and the kingdom of the Eternal City was rebuilt by the hands and in the style of man. The Wyt King tore down the Tree-Throne of the Elfin Empresses and replaced it with a large square seat of black marble with the yellow rose of the One God etched upon its crown. The Wyt King had secretly converted to the Temple of the One God after *experiencing* the holiness of the Tetrarchs' divinity. He forsook the Ring of a Hundred Souls, placing it deep within a hidden vault at the heart of the Palace of Silver Light. The majority of people continued to worship the Old Gods, despite the conversion of their king, but they never looked down upon their blessed ruler for his beliefs.

The Tetrarchs of the Temple of the One God came from Lemuria to dwell with the Wyt King in the Eternal City and soon a great temple was erected in the fifth district to honor the king's chosen deity. The Wizarding Clans remained powerful but the Old Nobility was slowly supplanted by a New Aristocracy of self-made men and favorites of the king. Theron Kalenti formally renounced his vows to the Wyt Robes, though they remained on friendly terms. He took a wife from the ranks of the New Aristocracy, a princess devoted to the One God and within a year was father to a healthy son, establishing the dynasty of the Wyts and ushering in the first patrilineal government to exist in Albion.

The Wyt King made allocations to the followers of the One God and placed them in key positions of power but he never turned his back on the powerful Old Religion. He yearned for peace and prosperity and showed ample kindness to all his subjects, proving to be a man of patience and virtue with a kind heart and a general concern for the wellbeing of others. Unfortunately, the world was not ready for his brand of leadership.

While the kingdom of Albion was rebuilt by the Wyt King, the Lady Rheis established her realm upon the tropical island of Ikaria in the violent Southern Sea. She raised the Green City of Itheria at the heart of the rainforest and was joined by many who wished to live as it had been before the wars with the Black Prince, in supplication to the Old Gods and their elfin emissaries. The power of the Autumn Crown was always at work, weaving powerful enchantments of protection so that none might enter Ikaria fostering hatred in their hearts. The world was vastly changed and fell into its new traditions, forgetting the power and glory of Elfkind and slowly falling towards darkness. No sooner had Elfkind been vanquished then a withered old gnomish-man living in the deeps of the Wynterlande Forest began plotting in the shadows...

The Lady and her Lies

Long, long ago, in the Eternal City of Atlantis there lived the Lord and Lady Dernevariost. Lord Dernevariost was a man of great power and prestige but was cold and callous towards his beautiful young wife. Lady Dernevariost had spent the three years of their marriage in almost complete isolation, taking up the seat at her spindle just after breakfast and staying there until the ringing of the noontime bells. She was deeply unhappy and her only solace were the long rides she would take on her mare, Solara, during the hot days of the year.

It was on one of her afternoon sojourns that she came across a small clearing in the middle of a dense forest where an athletic young man was sunbathing near a pond. He was completely naked, the perfect contours of his muscular body darkened to a high yellow and clean-shaven so that not even his man-parts bore the tufts of hair common in the men of the Atland. *Perhaps he is a mirage conjured by the faerie people,* the Lady Dernevariost thought to herself as she dismounted from Solara and moved closer to the pond. The young man stirred slightly as she approached but he gave no inclination that he knew she was there. He continued to rest his head on a small mound of peat moss, lost in some deep and distant dream.

"I know you're there," he finally said without opening his eyes, "I've seen you riding this way before…do you live nearby?"

The young man made no attempt to cover his genitals as he propped himself up on his elbows to look at the Lady. His eyes were of the deepest blue. The Lady felt like she was floating on the calm Western Sea as she stared into their depths. He smiled gently as his member began to grow. The Lady turned away with a start, covering her eyes with the scarf she wore over her shoulders as her face turned several shades of red. She was not accustomed to nudity but a part of her wanted to strip off her clothes and join the young man in his tanning. However, that thought was quickly fleeting as she recovered her senses and remembered her place. She was a woman of breeding who should never rightly find herself in such a compromising situation.

"You shouldn't be so forward, young man," she said bluntly, "I am a highborn woman, the Lady to his Lordship of Dernevariost and I do not think it proper to see you in such a state. Quickly now, tell me your name and what it is you do in these parts."

"Why?" he said playfully, "Are you going to report me to the local magistrates?"

"I have half a mind to do exactly that," countered the Lady coldly, inadvertently dropping her scarf and allowing her eyes to roam towards the young man's stiffening member. She had never seen a fully erect penis before. She thought it more beautiful than she was anticipating. Lord Dernevariost seldom came to the Lady's bed and, when he did he insisted they remain fully clothed. He would place her face down on the bed, remove her underwear, slip his manhood from his breeches and force it inside her with the sensuality of an ape. The entire affair typically lasted only minutes. When he was done the Lord would remove himself from inside her, cough twice, as though he had something lodged in his throat, and then leave the room. There was no romance and no foreplay, just the raw and unbearable act itself.

"I am called Gyrdhan," said the young man, breaking the Lady's trance, "I am a shepherd on a nearby farmstead…Would you like me to show you?"

What he was interested in showing her were not the fields where he spent his days herding sheep. He was far more interested in demonstrating his virility as a specimen of youthful perfection. He moved like a tiger stalking its morning meal as he came so close to the Lady she could smell him, a mixture of musk, body odor, and wool. He stroked himself as he reached out to gently touch her breasts. She allowed his hand to linger for only a split second as he fingered her nipple through the soft silk of her riding gown before her curiosity gave way to fear and she recoiled. She pushed him backward with such fierceness he almost fell to the ground.

"You dare to touch me?" she yelled, "I am a noblewoman and you, you are a peasant."

"Your words say that you don't want it," smiled Gyrdhan, "but your eyes betray you, m'Lady."

Gyrdhan pulled the Lady into his arms and kissed her passionately. For a moment it seemed she would push him away and run. Instead, she wrapped her arms around him and together they returned to the clover patch that had been serving as Gyrdhan's bed. The Lady slipped off her riding gown and her undergarments to expose her taut body and full breasts as Gyrdhan placed his head between her thighs and kissed her quinny, driving her to the edge of a mighty orgasm. When he replaced his tongue with his throbbing member, the Lady cried out in pain and pleasure, arching her back to allow for full penetration as Gyrdhan bucked like a stag in the rut. For nearly three hours they laid there next to the pond becoming familiar with all the secret places of each other's bodies before the sun began to drop beyond the trees, casting twilight shadows upon the clearing. The Lady stood, replaced her clothing and called her horse.

"Will I see you again?" she asked after mounting Solara.

"I'll come to this spot in the second hour of the afternoon every day," replied Gyrdhan.

"As will I," replied the Lady.

The next morning Lady Dernevariost rose with the sun and rode to the nearby Temple of the Moon to see her closest friend. Sister Renna was a Priestess of the Veil avowed to the service of the Triple Goddess and was the only person besides Lord Dernevariost that the Lady saw regularly. The Lady found Renna harvesting tomatoes in the gardens south of the temple. She was dressed in the plain multilayered robes of the priestesses and her face was covered by a thin purple veil. The Lady only recognized Renna because of the small silver brooch she wore over her left breast, a keepsake the Lady had given to her two years before.

"My Lady Dernevariost," said Renna, catching sight of her friend, "what a pleasant surprise. What brings you to the temple on such a fine spring morning?"

"I thought I might pray at the altar of the Mother," replied the Lady, "and I wanted to speak to you."

"Why don't we go to the Autumn Courtyard," said Renna, sensing the urgency in her friend's voice, "it's never in use at this time of year."

Renna led the Lady out of the vegetable gardens to a stone pathway running throughout the compound of the Temple of the Moon. They passed the Sacred Well and the altar of the Virgin Huntress before entering a grove of ancient oak trees growing very close together. At the heart of the grove stood a circle of massive stone monoliths surrounding a fountain springing up from the earth, forming a babbling brook trickling down a nearby hill and into the dense woods beyond.

"I have to tell you something Renna but you must promise not to judge," said the Lady once they were seated.

"It's not my place to judge," smiled Renna, "my role as a priestess is to advise and to listen."

"I met someone," blurted out the Lady.

"Someone?" asked Renna.

"His name is Gyrdhan…"

"How well have you come to know this Gyrdhan?"

When the Lady failed to answer, Renna stood and began pacing around the stone circle, her hands placed firmly upon her waist, her body language betraying her discontent.

"How many times have you slept with him?" asked Renna bluntly, "How many, Nerys?"

It came as a shock for Lady Dernevariost to hear her given name, even from Renna. The society of Atlantis was dominated by a rigid aristocracy which prevented those of lesser status from addressing highborn individuals by their informal given names. The caste system of the ancients had been abolished by the Wyt King who created a new formal aristocracy.

"Just once," replied Nerys.

"Do you intend to see him again?"

"Yes, yes I do...I have never felt so alive, Renna, and I want to know him better..."

"Then you must tell his Lordship," said Renna, "you must ask him to forgive you for your indiscretion and create a petition for divorce. The law of the land will support your right to dissolve your marriage..."

"And will the law protect me from my husband's wrath? He will kill me if I tell him what I've done."

"Tell me, Nerys...Have you taken up the Yellow Rose of the One God, or are you still a follower of the Old Religion?"

"You know I serve the Old Gods," said the Lady.

"Then you must confess what you have done...all wrongs that we do in this life must be made right before our final breath..."

"I cannot tell him," cried the Lady.

"The only alternative will be to lie and lies are the provenance of the darkness. Understand this, Nerys, for I will say it only once. Lies belong to that fourth moon goddess of which we never speak. She will allow your lies to blossom for only as long as they serve her. Then she will cut them off at the stem, exposing you for a coward and a deceiver."

"I do not begrudge you your love," added Renna sympathetically, "if that is truly what you feel for this Gyrdhan. But I must counsel you to respect your new love enough to cut the old one loose with honesty and grace."

Lady Dernevariost respected Renna's opinions but she was not prepared to follow her advice. Renna did not know Lord Dernevariost the same way as the Lady. He was far colder and crueler when he thought no one could see him berating and abusing his young wife. The Lady decided to kneel at the altar of the Mother and pray for guidance from the goddess she always believed was listening. She entered the sanctuary of the Mother at the heart of the temple, stripping off her clothes and bathing in the sacred waters before kneeling at the gigantic statue of a full-figured woman holding a dove in her hands, its wings spreading to take flight. The Lady closed her eyes, breathing deep the heavily scented air and seeking the place within herself where she could hear the goddess speak. She expected to hear the soft, reassuring tones of her own inner voice echoing in her mind but was instead greeted by a hard, shrill voice she had never heard before. Since she had never heard the words of the goddess before, she was a little frightened.

"You are right to worry, child," said the voice, *"I have seen your deepest fears and believe them to be founded...one small lie will not bring harm to you and will surely save your life...if you tell Dernevariost the truth, he will kill you."*

The Lady opened her eyes in shock, her skin as pale as the white marble of the mother's statue. She didn't know whether it was truly the Mother speaking within her mind but her words had a deep impact nonetheless. She rose from the altar and rushed out of the temple, mounting her horse and riding away as fast as Solara could carry her. She resolved that she would not tell Lord Dernevariost the truth but neither would she give up her new lover. She had but one choice. Ignoring the advice of her dearest friend she began to spin an elaborate tale to explain her absences from home every afternoon.

For the first two weeks after her visit to the Temple of the Moon, the Lady saw Gyrdhan every day without having to utter a single falsity. Lord Dernevariost was preoccupied by his monetary pursuits and rarely spent time with the Lady on a routine basis but even he began to grow suspicious as his wife continued to disappear. He was not accustomed to the Lady venturing out for hours at a time. She went for a horseback ride every afternoon but these were typically short, leaving her plenty of time to return home and dress for dinner. These days she barely made it back before the Lord went to bed.

"My Lady Wife," said the Lord one morning after unexpectedly joining the Lady for breakfast, "the servants have been whispering about your long absences from home...I am not one to listen to gossip but when it concerns the honor of my household I must ask. Where have you been going lately?"

"I have taken up the needle," she lied.

Needlepoint was a common pastime amongst the noblewomen of the Atland. It was a time when they came together at the Great Hall in the seventh district to gossip while slowly embroidering doilies and silken handkerchiefs for their husbands. The Lady had never taken a liking to these gatherings. She was not one to gossip, seeing it as a contradiction to her faith. Now she was willing to make her husband think she had become obsessed with the activity for her own self-preservation.

For many days the Lady's deception was a success, giving her the freedom to see Gyrdhan each day, falling in love with him more and more with each visit. Unfortunately, as fate would have it, a visiting noblewoman came to the Dernevariost home with her husband to petition the Lord for funds to save their small estate. During the course of their conversation, the Lord broached the subject of the needlepoint gatherings. The visiting lady was utterly confused, explaining the gathering had not met in the weeks spent observing the Beltane season. Lord Dernevariost was overcome by his suspicions as the following morning the Lady was once again joined at breakfast by her husband. Lord Dernevariost ate in silence, staring coldly at his wife until they were both done eating.

"We had visitors yesterday afternoon," said the Lord, "Lord and Lady Pekkala came to ask for gold to save their house...I'm sure you're on familiar terms with the Lady Pekkala since she is the leader of your needling circle."

The Lady knew that the Lord had discovered her falsehood, her legs beginning to shake slightly.

"I must tell you the truth, my Lord," she said, "I didn't really take up the needle. I only said I had because I knew you would be angry if you knew the truth…I've been visiting the Temple of the One God."

"You, visiting the Tetrarchs?" he asked, "I was under the impression that your devotion to the Old Religion was unyielding."

"It was but, as of late, I have been pondering the True Mysteries. I must say there are some very interesting philosophes embedded within them but I know that you aren't fond of the Tetrarchs, so I lied. I'm very sorry…"

"It's true that I'm not one of the 'True Believers' but I would never begrudge you the opportunity to explore your faith," said the Lord, "I just wish you would've been honest with me."

Lord Dernevariost excused himself from the table, leaving the lady to wonder if he had actually believed her newest deception. In truth he had not. For the three years of their marriage the Lady had shunned the Tetrarchs with absolute indifference, stating again and again that she would never abandon the teachings of the Temple of the Moon or the Old Religion, being born of the ancient bloodlines of the Atland.

Two days after their second breakfast, Lord Dernevariost decided to visit the Temple of the One God in the fifth district of the city, the only one of its kind in Atlantis at the time. He feigned a desire to donate a large sum of gold to the Tetrarchs as tithing for his wife's newfound devotion. He met personally with the Supreme Tetrarch, a man called Caros IV, and was not shocked to learn that the Tetrarchs had never seen Lady Dernevariost within the walls of their temple. Lord Dernevariost was outraged and hatched a plan to catch his wife in her secret dealings, convinced beyond a shadow of a doubt that she was hiding something terrible.

For a third time Lord Dernevariost joined his wife at breakfast, dining on boiled eggs, boar meat, and fresh fruit gathered from the orchards of the nearby gardens. He allowed her to finish her meal before he spoke.

"Tell me, dear wife, will you be visiting the Tetrarchs again this afternoon?"

"Of course," she said, "Why do you ask?"

"I thought I might send you with some gold. It is not proper for you to attend congregation without paying a formal tithing to the Tetrarchs."

Lord Dernevariost wished to confirm that his wife would be venturing off again that afternoon so he might follow her. He had his fastest horse saddled, waiting in the stables until he saw the Lady riding off into the forest. He waited a few minutes before setting out after her. He made sure to stay hidden in the underbrush, moving stealthily on a horse light of foot, until he came to the clearing at the heart of the woods where Gyrdhan was lying naked by the pond.

The Lord watched his wife dismount from Solara, pull off her riding gown and her undergarments, and join Gyrdhan on the ground, allowing him to fuck her with such force that she screamed like a wild savage. When they were finished she wrapped herself in Gyrdhan's arms and went to sleep. Before acting rashly in anger, Lord Dernevariost decided to ride back to his estate and prepare for the return of his wife. A few hours later, the Lady arrived home to find the head housekeeper waiting in the foyer with a message from the Lord.

"His Lordship has gone to the Palace to hold an audience with the Wyt King," said the housekeeper, "he shall return tomorrow afternoon and has asked that you join him for an early dinner in the formal banquet hall...he believes you may have something to celebrate."

The Lady was astounded that her husband wished to dine in the banquet hall. During the course of their marriage they had only once eaten in that enormous room and that was the night of their wedding feast. The following day she decided not to visit Gyrdhan. She would have had difficulty returning home in time to eat with Lord Dernevariost. Instead she visited the markets to purchase a new gown that she wore to dinner. Her husband was already seated at the enormous table dressed in his finest robes. They ate five courses in complete silence before the staff delivered dessert on two large platters covered by shiny silver lids.

"I do hope you will enjoy the dessert," said the Lord, "I had it prepared especially for you."

The Lady removed the lid on the platter, expecting to see a puff cake or chocolate mousse before dropping it on the floor in horror. There upon the plate was the severed head of her lover, resting in a pool of warm blood. Her face turned pale white and her eyes filled with tears as she stared down at all that remained of the man she had come to love very deeply.

"Did you really think I would allow you to make a fool of me without suffering serious consequences?" said the Lord, "Don't you know the nature of lies, wife. They will only ever betray you, just as you have betrayed me..."

"Do you mean to kill me too?" asked the Lady.

"No," said the Lord, "I think I have dealt you a far greater blow than death...I can see on your tortured face how much he meant to you. It's a shame you won't have the chance to be together again."

"You are no longer my wife," he continued, "Go now from my house and never return...take nothing with you. It all belongs to me."

The Lady did as she was instructed, walking away from her home with tears soaking her face. She could think of only one place to go and made her way on foot to the Temple of the Moon to see Sister Renna, intending to take the vows of the Priestesses of the Veil and live the rest of her life in quiet devotion to the Mother but, when she arrived, she was greeted by shuns from the Sisters, all of whom turned their backs upon her. Even Renna would not look in her direction.

"I wish to take the vows," said the Lady.

"I warned you about lying," replied Renna, "you turned your back on the Mother…you are disgraced. You may never take the vows and may never again come here to worship…I hope it was worth it, losing everything because you were too cowardly to tell the truth…I pray this experience has taught you a valuable lesson."

The Treachery of Princess Nerys

At the height of the Golden Age of Atlantis, the throne was occupied by the second Wyt King, Eathon Kalenti. Known to the people as the *Peace King*, his desire to preserve the ancient law of the land at all costs was paramount. He was a congregant at the Temple of the One God but allowed the followers of the Old Religion to follow their traditions without persecution. As a sign of solidarity with the Old Gods and because of his personal lust, he took the Lady Nerys Sanva as his wife. Nerys was devoted to the Triple Goddess of the Temple of the Moon and her presence at court provided the Old Nobility with a voice near to the Wyt King. Unfortunately, Nerys' benevolent and compassionate persona was a cover for something dark and dangerous hiding beneath.

Queen Nerys had long before been wounded deeply when the only man she ever loved was murdered by her jealous husband before casting her out into the night, disgraced and alone. She tried to turn to the Sisterhood of the Moon but they shunned her for her dishonest adultery. In that pitiful and broken moment, Nerys turned to the only power still willing to embrace her, the malevolent Nameless Goddess, called the Poisoner, the Destroyer of Dreams, and the Darkmoon Deceiver. For months, Nerys bled herself at the Well of Shadows and sacrificed wild hares in supplication before the Nameless Goddess finally rose from the dark waters of the deep well, materializing as the watery silhouette of an ageless woman, a ghostly apparition that cast an eerie shadow across the island as she grew to her full and terrifying stature.

"*Long have you laid before my waters,*" said the Nameless Goddess, "*but you have delivered no sacrifice worthy of my attention.*"

"What must I give?" pleaded Nerys, "I will do anything for the power to seek revenge against that bastard I called my husband and that upstart bitch, Renna, the Pretender of the Veil.

"Deliver to me the virility of a youth cut off by your own hand and I will give you the power which you seek."

Nerys stayed true to her word, journeying to the nearby village of Tarethar. There she found a youth all too eager to follow her into the Marshland Forest, hoping to lay naked with her in carnal lust. He ran after her like a stag following a doe in heat until they came to the island at the heart of the forest, where stood the Well of Shadows. Nerys took the youth into her arms, stripped him of his clothes and threw him down on the ground, mounting him and slipping his manhood inside her. She yelled out as she approached the edge of orgasm, her body shaking with ecstasy. She drew forth a knife from beneath the blanket and used it to cut off the young man's hard penis with one firm swipe of her wrist. The youth screamed in agony as blood spewed forth from the fresh wound between his legs. Nerys stood over the youth, staring coldly as the last of his blood escaped his seizing body. When she was sure he was dead, she spit on his corpse and dropped his severed member into the well. The moment it hit the water there was a bright flash of green light and the Nameless Goddess appeared before Nerys, not as a watery silhouette, but as a woman of flesh and blood with skin as flawless as marble and wild hair the color of ravens. Her red eyes narrowed with a hateful glare and, when she spoke, her voice was as cold as ice.

"I have been trapped in that well for 500 years," said the Nameless Goddess, "waiting for the sacrifice that would finally set me free. I am now in your debt, daughter of Arimon…you wish to have the power to exact revenge against those who have wronged you and I will not deny you that but, why only your wretched husband and that backstabber you called your friend? All men should suffer, especially the one you call the Wyt King."

"Why the Wyt King?"

"That is my business…all you need be concerned with is playing your part. I will teach you all you need to know to have your revenge and, in return, you will steal something for me, something once precious to the Wyt King, though it hasn't been seen in many years."

Nerys had little choice but to become the Nameless Goddess' student. Nerys learned all the ways of the darkness in the Art from her new mentor. For five years, she dwelt in the darkness of the Marshland Forest and devoted herself to her studies. She learned to evoke pain in others remotely and to plant insidious desires into the minds of men. She learned the art of the glamour and how to wrap herself in the shadows so she might walk unseen amongst others. She learned the spells of famine and pestilence, to invoke those devilish spirits called demons, and to cast curses of varying terrifying effect. The only power she had trouble mastering was the Sight. She had zero ability to see future events, not in her mind's eye nor by scrying into a mirror. Still, her powers grew to an impressive degree and, at last, she set out to enact her revenge, going first to the large country estate of her estranged husband.

Nerys' former husband, Lord Dernevariost, had grown very frail by the time she returned to his home just outside the walls of the Eternal City. He didn't have the strength to stand as she entered the Great Hall of his country mansion and approached him, still young and vibrant, being just thirty years of age. She was dressed in the finest crimson gown embroidered with pearls and adorned herself with a silver tiara cradling a large ruby. The Lord didn't recognize her at first. He thought she might be one of the noblewomen from the Temple of the One God come to provide for his earthly needs in his final hours. It wasn't until she sat down in the chair opposite him that he realized who she was.

"I never thought I would see your face again," said the Lord.

"You didn't think I'd let you die without coming to pay my respects," replied Nerys, "and I wanted to thank you…"

"For what?" wheezed the Lord, "for exposing you as a duplicitous little whore and liar?"

"No, I wasn't referring to that particularly unpleasant moment. I meant for cutting me free from your influence…if you hadn't kicked me out into the cold with nothing, I would never have found my way to the True Mother. I would never have embraced the darkness."

"Forgive me for not congratulating you, whore. Leave my house this second or I will ring for the groundskeeper and have him throw you out on your ass again."

"You were always such an eloquent man. Before I leave I want to show you something…"

Lord Dernevariost tried to stand and walk away but, as she had been sitting there, Nerys was weaving a subtle unspoken spell to paralyze him. He couldn't move a single muscle until she lifted her curse. He sat there helplessly watching as Nerys pulled a small wooden box from the beaded satchel she carried at her waist. The box was marked with a large black circle connected to the symbol of the Sacred Feminine and, when she flipped open the lid, the room was instantly filled with a pungent, unbearable odor, as though someone left a batch of onions to rot in the summer heat.

"Have you ever heard of the Nightshade Root?" asked Nerys, but Lord Dernevariost didn't answer, "it's said to be the deadliest poison to exist in Albion but it's the way it works that's truly magnificent…it starts by inducing violent seizures that leave the head pounding. Then it starts working on the organs, shutting them down one by one, starting with the lungs and finishing with the brain…the entire process takes more than an hour. I've been told the victim remains conscious the whole time, experiencing every excruciating moment. I can't wait to see if it's true…"

Nerys stood and walked over to Lord Dernevariost, still frozen in his chair. She forced his mouth open and shoved the entire contents of the box down his throat. He sputtered and coughed as the Nightshade worked its way to his stomach, working its foul magic instantly. He frothed and foamed at the mouth as he shook so violently it seemed he would fall from his chair. For twenty minutes, he endured seizure after seizure before his lungs began to burn, desperately and hopelessly gasping for air.   From then, the degeneration was rapid. Within fifteen minutes, he was dead.

"What a shame," said Nerys, "I had hoped it would last longer."

The death of Dernevariost brought Nerys some satisfaction but she still yearned for more. She went that same night to the nearby Temple of the Moon to see her once closest friend, Sister Renna, to call her out on her betrayal so many years before. Nerys wrapped herself in shadows and entered the House of Priestesses just south of the temple. She found Renna sleeping on a feather mattress near the fire. Renna had aged a lot in the few years since they had last met. Her hair was turning gray and her face was worn.

"I know you're there," said Renna without opening her eyes, "I felt you enter the grounds…"

"Of course you did," sneered Nerys as she made herself visible.

"You have changed much, my old friend," said Renna.

"Don't call me that," spat Nerys, "you are nothing…I have only one true friend."

"Yes, I am aware of your teacher. She walks again in the living world but her strength has not returned to her…"

"It will in time. Until then, I will be her strength and serve her in all her needs."

"I am sorry that I failed you, Nerys. I acted like a stupid child…I didn't understand the true meaning of the Mysteries then…but I do now."

"You think you can just apologize and it'll make everything okay?" laughed Nerys, "that you can escape your fate by simply uttering a single word of kindness?"

"I have seen my future, Nerys, and I do not die by your hand."

"Perhaps your visions misled you."

"Perhaps," said Renna.

"It makes no difference...you will die tonight, Renna, that I can guarantee."

Nerys pulled a handful of shiny black dust from her satchel and threw it at Renna. As it floated through the air, the dust took on a life of its own. It circled around Renna like a vulture seeking the dead flesh of a recently fallen carcass but, before it made its final descent, Renna spoke a single powerful word and caused a magnificent golden aura to materialize around her, preventing the deadly dust from coming any closer. Renna smiled as Nerys pulled a makeshift cloth doll from her satchel and retrieved the sharp pin she was using to hold up her hair. She muttered a terrible curse under her breath before jabbing the pin into the doll. As Nerys drove the pin deeper, Renna put her hand in front of her like she was blocking something from hitting her in the face. This time, a silver light erupted from her hand and Nerys doubled over in pain. The enchantment had caused Nerys curse to backfire and she looked down to see a large gash above her right breast oozing blood the same color as her gown.

"You cannot win," said Renna.

"I will find a way," screamed Nerys as she ran out of the House of Priestesses and into the night. She wrapped her wound with a piece of her gown and applied constant pressure but it would not stop bleeding. By the time she arrived at the Well of Shadows she was nearly dead. The Nameless Goddess healed her wound and put her to bed in the ruined tower, feeding her broth full of vegetables and warm milk from a mountain goat. When Nerys was finally recovered, the Nameless Goddess called her to the well.

"I see your revenge is only half realized," she said, "but it matters not...I have waited long enough. You will now do what you promised and seek what I need from the Wyt King."

"I haven't killed Renna yet," replied Nerys.

"No, you haven't, and you won't. Renna is too powerful."

"Then I need more power," sneered Nerys.

"If you do what I ask of you, I will show you how to gain greater power than you could possibly imagine."

"What must I do?" asked Nerys, easily seduced by the Nameless Goddess' promise of power.

"The Wyt King will be holding court at the Summer Palace, in the city of Tansapar," explained the Nameless Goddess, "which is fortuitous since what you seek is likely hidden there…it is a ring of true silver set with a large ruby encircled by tiny diamonds. The last time it was seen was at the Wyt King's coronation. He supposedly gave the ring to the Tetrarchs of the One God after he was crowned but I believe this was a smokescreen meant to make the people believe he no longer had the ring in his possession. Whatever the case, he has not openly worn it since."

"And what's so important about this ring?" asked Nerys.

"Haven't you been listening? The ring is very important to the king…to steal it would deal a terrible blow to his ego and allow me the opportunity to enter his nightmares and manipulate him from afar. Look for the ring in a vault or hidden chamber within the Summer Palace…enlist the aid of anyone you trust. Just do what you must to bring me that ring."

Nerys left the Marshland Forest right away, making her way to the village of Tarethar where she hired a coach to take her to Tansapar. The port of Tansapar was a thriving metropolis situated on the Bay of Alfalas in the east of the Atland. Home to noteworthy merchants, writers, and musicians, Tansapar had become the jewel of the nation, outshining even the Eternal City in splendor. The Wyt King, Theron Kalenti, was responsible for the growth of Tansapar into the urban hotspot it had become. He spent the majority of the year living at the Summer Palace and encouraged his *New Nobility* to buy the newly built and enormous villas springing up around the palace grounds while the Eternal City was neglected and left to the authority of powerful land barons.

Nerys knew enough about Theron Kalenti to know that she would need to present herself with absolute evocativeness and personal majesty in order to draw his attention and gain access to his ring. She dressed in the most magnificent purple gown she owned, with a thin white veil thrown over her hair and various jewels adorning her fingers, neck and ears. She wore a diadem of bronze and bathed herself in rosewater before entering the Summer Palace to see the Wyt King.

The palace was filled with courtiers from the four corners of Albion, gathered to celebrate the birthday of the king's only son and heir, Prince Eathon Kalenti. Even amongst the massive throngs of people, Nerys drew the eye of every adult male in the great hall. She was a rare beauty who had blossomed in her thirties. Her hair was a deep red and her eyes the color of a tropical lagoon. The Wyt King saw her the moment she entered and followed her with his eyes.

"Who's that?" he asked his steward.

"I have no idea, your Grace," replied the steward.

"Find out," said the king.

The steward rushed off into the crowd towards Nerys.

"The Wyt King would like to meet you, my Lady," said the steward after reaching Nerys.

Nerys followed him back to a raised balcony connected to the main floor of the hall by a grand marble staircase. The Wyt King was seated leisurely at a table, dining on fresh fruit with bread and honey, while his son, Prince Eathon, stood behind him with a cask of wine. The Wyt King was nearing his fifties and had grown rather fat in his decade ruling Atlantis, a pale comparison to the athletic and attractive man he had been in his youth. He was a warm and jovial man prone to outbursts of laughter and smiled gingerly as Nerys bowed at his feet.

"Your Grace," said the steward, "may I present…"

"The Lady Nerys Sanva of Dernevariost," said Nerys.

"It is a pleasure to meet you, my Lady," said the Wyt King, "this is my son, Eathon."

Prince Eathon nodded at Nerys from behind his father's chair. He was mesmerized by her rare beauty and felt his heart skip a beat as she smiled at him warmly. Prince Eathon had just turned eighteen years old that day and his hormones were aching for release. His father meant to marry him to a foreign princess but Eathon was stubborn and unwilling to take a bride not of his choosing. He was infatuated with Nerys. They spent the rest of the afternoon together, drinking wine, listening to music, and walking through the large gardens outside the palace. Nerys allowed the prince to touch her lightly and to whisper in her ear. She flirted and plied him with generous portions of wine to ensure that whatever qualms he may feel about her would disappear. When they reached the fountains at the edge of the royal estate and Nerys was sure Eathon was drunk, she insisted they sit on a bench under the boughs of an apple tree. They talked about Eathon's childhood and a fictitious youth invented by Nerys before she mentioned the magnificence of the Summer Palace.

"Tell me, sweet prince," she said, "are there any hidden places we might explore? You know, secret passageways, ancient crypts, hidden vaults, that sort of thing. I love those kinds of places, with relics and artifacts from the past. Do you know of any in the palace?"

"I can think of a few," said the drunken prince.

Eathon took Nerys to a small library with a large fireplace which slid away to reveal a narrow stone passage leading into the hidden parts of the palace. They visited a series of crypts beneath the east wing, filled with the mummified remains of long dead Elfkind. Eathon showed Nerys the aqueducts and secret wine cellars and he took her to see a storeroom filled with ancient portraits and sculptures fashioned by hands long since passed from the world. The tour took hours and when they emerged the palace was quieting as the courtiers returned to their homes in the city.

"That was wonderful," said Nerys, "but is there nowhere else? Maybe a place filled with treasure?"

Eathon squinted his eyes for a second, as though he were trying to hold in unwanted bodily gases, before something dawned on him and he grabbed Nerys by the hand. They raced up stairway after stairway, through corridor after corridor, until they came to a massive set of redwood doors. Eathon looked back and forth several times before cracking the door and slipping inside. They were standing in a large room with an enormous feather bed set across from a large fireplace.

"This is my father's bedchamber," said Eathon, "he'd kill us if he knew we were in here."

"Then we'd best be quick," replied Nerys with a smile.

Eathon took her over to a dresser on the far wall and began turning one iron knob after another until the dresser popped off the wall like the lid of a jam jar, revealing a narrow archway leading to a small room on the other side. This room was filled with jewels of every shape, style, and form, from tiaras to necklaces, bracelets to rings, all situated around a small glass box containing a ring of true silver set with a ruby encircled by tiny diamonds. Nerys had found what she was looking for.

"What's that?" asked Nerys, pointing to the ring in the box.

"Oh, that," said Eathon, "that's the Ring of a Hundred Souls…you can't tell anyone you saw it. It's not supposed to be here."

"The Ring of a Hundred what?"

"It's my father's magic ring…he used it to depose the Last Elfin Empress. It supposedly holds a hundred fallen souls in its ruby and makes its wielder super powerful. But I've never seen it working its magic before."

Nerys' eyes widened as she stared at the beautiful ring, finally understanding the Nameless Goddess' desire to own it. Nerys and Eathon left the hidden vault quickly and returned to the great hall below but Nerys returned that night, when the Wyt King was deep asleep, and entered the vault again. She stole the ring from its glass box and slipped it on her finger and she felt its power washing over her like a wave rising up from the sea to drown the shore. Her first act as wielder of the ring was to magically create a duplicate she placed inside the glass box before returning to the room provided to her by the Wyt King for the duration of her stay.

The next morning, she joined Prince Eathon for breakfast on the south terrace, overlooking the waters of the Bay of Alfalas. They talked more about her fictitious childhood and his own life before his father became king. When they were finished eating, Nerys took the prince's hand and quietly whispered a spell under her breath.

"Ydych chi eisiau i mi briodi," she said, *"a gwynedd i mi eich freniras."*

Eathon's eyes blurred for a moment as he fell into a daze. When he came to, he was looking at Nerys adoringly and spoke with gentle words meant to soothe and entice her.

"Marry me, Nerys," he said, "I won't be whole until you agree to be my bride...I must have you."

"And so you shall," said Nerys, "but there's something I must tend to before our wedding."

Nerys left the Summer Palace on the back of a prized white stallion, riding with great speed back to the Marshland Forest. She arrived at the Well of Shadows just as the sun was rising to its apex. The Nameless Goddess was waiting for her in the ruined tower. She jumped up and ran to meet Nerys like a child eager for affection.

"Did you get it?" asked the Nameless Goddess.

"Yes, but there's something I don't understand," said Nerys.

"What's that, my dear?"

"I don't understand why you didn't tell me the ring was magic...that it housed a hundred fallen souls and gave its wearer near limitless power. Were you afraid I wouldn't give the ring to you if I knew the truth of its magic? Did you think I would turn it against you?"

"The thought crossed my mind," said the Nameless Goddess. "You were right."

Nerys moved too quickly for the Nameless Goddess to counter, conjuring a powerful bolt of purple light that she hurtled towards the Nameless Goddess with the force of a train hitting a brick wall. The Nameless Goddess was pierced just above the heart and blood poured forth from the wound as she fell to her knees. For a moment she knelt there, staring at Nerys in disbelief, before a dark orb of black light materialized above her head. Nerys called to the black orb with her ring and it flew through the air to join with the other souls within the depths of the ruby.

"I knew you'd betray me!" shrieked the Nameless Goddess, "but I never thought you would steal my soul."

"I'm sorry, mistress," replied Nerys, "but I couldn't just give up the chance to make the ring more powerful. Not even for you."

The Nameless Goddess tried to stand but Nerys waved her hand, as though she were dismissing unwanted help, and the Nameless Goddess started shaking, as though she were about to explode. She fell, face down, and dissolved into a puddle on the ground. Moments later, she reappeared from the depths of the well as the watery silhouette she had been when Nerys first made her acquaintance.

"I am sorry," said Nerys, "and I promise you, mistress. One day I will find you another soul…"

"*Three,*" echoed the voice of the Nameless Goddess, "*this treachery will cost you three souls…and I warn you Nerys. I won't wait forever.*"

The following morning Nerys returned to Tansapar and marched into the Summer Palace, dressed in her finest gown of silver silk. She wore the ancestral makeup of the Atlandish tribes upon her face and adorned her brow with a tiara of silver and rubies. Upon her right ring finger, hidden beneath a velvet glove, she wore the Ring of a Hundred Souls, with the essence of the Nameless Goddess' soul trapped inside with the countless others pulled into the ring over the ages. All eyes were fixed on her as she made her way gracefully into the throne room and knelt at the feet of the first Wyt King.

"Your Grace," she said, "I have come here to humbly ask your permission to wed your son. He has asked me to be his bride and I have accepted. If it pleases you, my king, I would like to be your daughter."

"To have you in our family would be a blessing indeed," said the Wyt King, "You have my permission to marry my son."

Prince Eathon ran out from behind his father's throne and scooped Nerys into his arms, hugging her tightly and kissing her gently on the neck.

"I promise I will make you happier than you have ever been, my princess," said Eathon.

The preparations for the wedding took nearly three months. The couple was married in the Temple of the One God, though there was a High Priestess of the Triple Goddess present to administer the ancient rites of the Old Religion to Nerys. The Wyt King embraced his daughter-in-law with open arms and welcomed her into his House as she took the vows to stand as consort to Eathon forever and always abide his will. She was given the crown that was worn by Eathon's mother when she married the Wyt King and was presented to all the noblemen, both old and new, from the four corners of Albion. The whole of Albion rejoiced at the coming of a princess faithful to the Old Gods, celebrating with feasts and bonfires, everyone except a single Priestess of the Veil, who laid dying in her bed, struck down by a strange and painful fever after hearing a fell voice on the cold night wind cursing for her demise.

The Black Prince Returns

In the nine years when the power of the Witch-Queen reached into the four corners of Albion, there were few kingdoms in the living world remaining free of her tyranny. The Wynterlande Forest was one such place and there, amidst the tall evergreen trees, dwelt the gnomish-men called the Dunmors. The Dunmors were much smaller in stature than other men but were skilled hunters with strong arms and fast legs. They lived simple lives tending farms and hunting game in the southern groves of the forest. The largest of their villages was Beddlebern where dwelt young Tobin Nahas.

Tobin was always small, even by the standards of the Dunmors, and grew up with a sickly demeanor. While the other Dunmor children played hide and seek in the thickets of the forest, Tobin stayed indoors reading and playing kataskat, a game similar to chess but with a multilevel board and three sets of pieces. Tobin's father was disgusted by his son's physical inferiority, while his mother felt pity for him. They were both strong Dunmors who assumed their duties within the village upon reaching adulthood. Tobin's father was one of the hunters who went frequently into the deeps of the woods to hunt deer and other forest game. Tobin's mother was an apothecary with a deep knowledge of the medicinal plants growing within the Wynterlande. They were both well-respected within the village, making the meager personality of their only son all the harder to bear.

Tobin was fascinated with books and spent most of his time reading. He also liked to watch the other children outside playing amongst the trees, wishing he had the wherewithal to join them. He wished he had been born with the strength to run and to play and to be free but his fear was so great that it outweighed any of his secret desires. Someday he would gather the courage to become something greater but he did not know how or when, and his long days of loneliness weighed heavily on his mind.

One summer morning a few days after Tobin's seventeenth birthday, his parents approached him over breakfast to talk about his future. He had never really given it much thought.

"We have babied you long enough, Tobin, the time has come for you to grow up," said Tobin's father.

"We only want what's best for you," said his mother.

"I want you to be a man," added his father.

"It that really necessary, Halgan," said Tobin's mother.

"Yes," he replied, "I think it is…you have let him sit here in the dark with his books long enough, Ertyl. This afternoon, he will go with me on the hunt…and he's not coming back until he's killed his first stag."

"You really think he has the stamina for that?"

"We'll see, won't we?" said Tobin's father.

Tobin had no choice in the matter. That afternoon he journeyed away from Beddlebern for the first time, making his way into the heart of the ancient forest with his father, two other hunters, and each of their sons. Tobin was armed with an old spear, as were the other boys his age, while his father and the other hunters brandished swords the size of large knives. They were wearing buckskin tunics and carried small satchels filled with dried meat, water, and berries on their backs. Hunting trips sometimes lasted for weeks and the Dunmors often ventured far from home in search of their prey. Tobin was frightened as they entered the parts of the forest where the sun barely penetrated the boughs of the giant trees. It was cold, dark, and eerie. Tobin stayed on his father's heels and made a conscious effort to never look back. After hours of walking they stopped by the decaying remnants of an old cottage to camp for the night. Tobin's father built a roaring fire and they shared the bits of dried meat and berries from their satchels. Tobin tried to be brave but his imagination got the better of him. He barely slept and awoke to the dim light trickling through the branches of the trees, covered in cold dew that chilled him to the bone.

"Today you will become a man," said Tobin's father, clapping him hard on the back and smiling encouragingly.

"I won't fail you, father," replied Tobin.

"I know, son, just do your best…eventually you'll get the hang of it."

They set out without breakfast, moving further from home and deeper into the forest until they came upon a few does grazing in a nearby clearing. Tobin's father and the other hunters split up, stalking quietly towards the meadow. Tobin followed his father and tried to remain silent. They had just reached the bushes at the edge of the clearing when Tobin sneezed. The deer took off running, disappearing amidst the trees in a matter of seconds. Tobin looked away from his father, not able to take the disdain dripping from his face. They silently rejoined the other hunters and continued their trek. Tobin hung back for fear of being lectured and soon lost sight of the others.

Tobin panicked as he came to a particularly thick grove of evergreens growing on the shores of a little stream. Tobin couldn't tell if the hunters had crossed the stream or if they had continued onward along its banks. He decided to journey downstream, thinking that it might lead to a pond or marshy meadow the hunters would make their way towards in search of game. The dull glow of sunlight penetrating the forest canopy diminished as Tobin continued walking. If he was any kind of hunter, he could have tracked the others or, at the very least, set up camp and await their return. Unable to bear the fear any longer, Tobin sat down on a rock at the mouth of an old cave and began to cry.

"What's the matter, little one?" said an old man from behind Tobin. He jumped up and turned around, grabbing his old spear and holding it in front of him. An extremely old and frail Dunmor man was standing at the cave opening, holding himself up with a tiny wooden cane carved from a piece of old growth. The old man had a dusting of black hair growing from the top of his head and his eyebrows were so bushy Tobin could barely see his eyes. The old man was just as small as Tobin, if not a little smaller, with a big hump on his back. He had a weathered complexion and had green eyes that glowed like a shamrock caught in the light of the morning sun.

"I'm lost," replied Tobin, "I don't know how to get home because I can't track or hunt or do anything useful."

"I don't know about that," replied the old man, "everyone has something they're good at…you might not be a hunter but I'm sure you have your strengths."

"I have no strengths, only weakness."

"Then we will have to find something for you to be good at."

"What is your strength?" asked Tobin.

"I'm a wizard," replied the old man, "but, alas, my magic amulet was stolen from me long ago. Without it, I too am useless. If only I had the strength of youth, I would venture to the Red Tower and retrieve it myself…"

Tobin had never heard of a gnomish wizard. He had read the tales of the Old Religion and Elfkind, about the adventures of the Wandering Wizard and the Lady of the Green City. He was learned in the history of the outside world, though he also heard terrible stories about the Witch-Queen ruling beyond the forest. The idea of a living breathing wizard standing before him erased Tobin's fear as his inquisitive nature began to show.

"The Red Tower?" asked Tobin.

"It is a great spire that rises high into the heavens," said the old man, "four hours northeast of here, on the edge of the Wynterlande Forest. It is home to a wicked witch with enchanted mirrors that show her all the comings and goings in that part of the woods."

"You mean the Red Witch?" asked Tobin, "I've read stories about her…she's supposed to have the power to control fire and she likes to eat Dunmors for dinner…its forbidden for any to visit the northeast groves."

"Which is why I have yet to find someone to seek my amulet," said the old man sadly.

Tobin realized what he could do to make himself a hero in the eyes of the village and finally force his father to love him. Despite his fear and physical frailty, Tobin vowed to find a way to steal back the old gnomish wizard's amulet. Surely the only wizard he had ever known would be welcomed warmly by the other Dunmors, like a savior or a prophet, and Tobin would receive the same admiration.

"I will seek out your amulet," said Tobin, "though I will likely fail for I know not how to succeed."

"The Red Witch has a weakness," smiled the old man, "she, like all living things, must sleep. When she does, she is dead to the world. Wait until the moon reaches the highest point in the night sky and then enter by the back stair…Dunmors are naturally stealthy. I doubt you will be heard. My amulet will be in a jewelry box in her room, wherein lies the danger…if you make too much noise even the slumbering witch will know you are there."

"And what does your amulet look like?" asked Tobin.

"It is a large golden pendant the shape of a teardrop…and at its heart it cradles a large diamond that will glow with a dull orange light. It will be upon a long golden chain which cannot be removed and is engraved with runes of the Old Gods on its face and back."

"Look over there, do you see that trail?" continued the old man, pointing to a narrow dirt path winding through the nearby trees, "that is what remains of the Wynterlande Road…it will take you directly to the Red Tower…remember to wait until midnight before you enter. If you are successful you will have my undying gratitude and I will teach you a valuable lesson in the uses of magic."

Tobin took a deep breath and gathered what little courage he could muster before setting out northeast along the Wynterlande Road. He decided his father was searching for him after noticing he was missing but assumed that any anger he might feel towards Tobin for running off would be appeased by Tobin's gallant act of bravery. For four hours, Tobin kept to the road before emerging from the forest onto a wide, flat plane. In the distance, on the banks of a wide river, stood the Red Tower. It was the tallest building Tobin had ever seen, built from rare blocks of red marble inlayed with massive sheets of gold. It looked like an enormous wand fell from the heavens and stuck vertically into the earth. Tobin wondered who could have built something so exotic and amazing.

Tobin waited, hidden amongst an outcropping of rocks, until the sun set and the moon rose high into the sky. There was no light shining from the windows of the Red Tower. Near to midnight, Tobin decided the moment had come for him to enter. He found the doorway to the back stairs on the southern wall of the tower and entered without making a sound. The passage on the other side was completely dark. Tobin guessed the walls and floors were made from the same red marble as the exterior. Without a candle or torch, he had to rely on his acute hearing and sensitive touch to navigate the corridor. The back stairs were mere feet from the entrance. Tobin crawled up them like a mouse foraging for dinner, careful not to scrape the ground or allow his clothes to shuffle. He was petrified but his determination to succeed drove him to the wide landing at the top of the stairs and the single white door standing slightly ajar, with a soft golden glow coming from the room on the other side.

The Red Witch was laying upon a large feather bed, covered by a thin silk blanket and snoring softly. She was the size of a normal woman of the Atland and wore a cover over her eyes as she slept. Tobin crept into the room, able to fit through the opening without touching the partially opened door. The room was small and octagonal, furnished with only the bed, a large dresser, and a vanity in the corner atop which a candle was burning. Next to the candle sat a large wooden jewelry box embossed with shiny silver and colorful gemstones.

Tobin crept over to the vanity on his tiptoes as the Red Witch continued to snore quietly. He was careful not to disturb his surroundings and kept out of the candlelight. He tried the lid of the box but it was locked, requiring a small crystal key to open. Tobin read about crystalline locking mechanisms in one of his books and knew what the key would look like. It would be a long conical rod of crystal with a series of notches etched into one side. It could be any color but the size would be small, no larger than a toothpick and easily concealed. For a moment he was sure his mission had come to an end before he caught sight of a tiny rod of white crystal tied to the Red Witch's wrist with a pink ribbon. Tobin was overwhelmed by a desire to run out the door and never look back but he conjured his courage and made his way silently to the edge of the witch's bed. She turned from her back to her side as he approached, making him jump slightly and to halt where he stood shaking.

Tobin reached out his stubby fingers and began to untie the ribbon holding the key to the witch's wrist but she flipped again, causing him to be tossed over her and onto the bed. He laid there completely still just inches from the undisturbed Red Witch. He could feel her warm breath on his face. It smelled of fresh meat and wine. As she exhaled a particularly loud snore, Tobin rolled off the bed and crouched on the floor in case the sound of the sheets rustling caused the witch to wake. When he was sure she was still asleep, he crawled around the bed where her wrist was dangling loosely off the edge. This time he was successful in unbinding the knot, releasing the key into his waiting hands. He rushed back over to the box and unlocked it to reveal an exquisitely rare and undeniably old diamond amulet etched with unique, lyrical runes.

Tobin grabbed the chain the amulet was fastened to and yanked it from the box, momentarily forgetting about the candle sitting next to the jewelry box. As he stuffed the amulet in his inside pocket he accidentally knocked the candle over. It hit the floor with a crash and the Red Witch sat straight up, pulling the mask from her eyes to expose her beautiful and flawless white face. She looked at Tobin with narrowed eyes, not noticing the partially open lid of the jewelry box.

"I have come to offer my services to the great Red Witch," said Tobin, thinking quickly, "I was told by your manservant downstairs that I should come immediately to inquire about a position within your household."

"I am afraid that the work to be done around here would be too strenuous for a gnome, my little friend," she said sweetly, "but I don't think that's the real reason you have come here..."

"I swear to you that it is."

"Then I must respectively decline your request and ask you to leave my home at once," said the Red Witch as Tobin made his way back to the door. It wasn't until he was outside in the passageway that he heard the Red Witch scream in frustration and knew she had discovered the amulet was missing. He ran as fast as his little legs would carry him, bolting down the back stairs and out the door before he heard a disincarnate voice carried on a powerful wind.

"*Come back,*" said the Red Witch, "*you know not what you do.*"

Tobin darted into a thicket of brambles, using them as a thorny causeway to return him to the woods. Once back inside the forest he traveled along the edge of the Wynterlande Road, determined to stay out of sight. The sun began to rise and the forest was filled with a dull twilight glow as Tobin made the last of his journey, returning safely to the cavern where the old gnomish wizard was waiting patiently on a rock outside. He perked up as he saw Tobin appear from behind a large tree.

"Did you get it?" asked the old man.

Tobin had just produced the amulet from the inside pocket of his jacket when there came an explosion of fire and the Red Witch appeared from within its depths. Without uttering a word she held out her hand, like she was expecting to be handed something and the amulet shot furlong out of Tobin's grip. But the old man was able to wrap his withered fingers around the chain. The moment he did he began to transform. He grew as tall as a Norn Giant with a muscular body and long, angular face. His brown hair was thick and long and he bore a small beard upon his chin. His eyes turned to the color of lava as he furrowed his brow. He slipped the chain holding the amulet around his neck and bellowed forth a monstrous laugh. The Red Witch backed away but the newly transformed man grabbed her with an invisible hand, squeezing her so hard her ribs cracked.

"You're too late, Leanida," laughed the man.

"Do what you will to me, Ragnar," whispered the Red Witch, "there will always be someone to take my place…this is far from over."

Ragnar smiled maniacally as he turned from the Red Witch to face Tobin cowering behind a rock.

"I do believe I promised you a lesson in magic," said Ragnar, "and I always honor my promises…"

Ragnar wrapped his hands around his amulet, causing the Red Witch to rise up into the air like she was suspended from invisible wires. She rose over teen feet in the air as Ragnar began to chant a terrible spell, filled with hatred and loathing, one that echoed through the forest with the power of a gale-force wind.

"*Azarog ashta nemethar hanas,*" he said, "*Twyregh lara mon thaas.*"

The effect of the spell was immediate. The Red Witch was torn apart limb by limb as though some giant predator had pounced upon her in midair, pulling off her legs one at a time, followed by her arms and then her head.

Ragnar was far from finished with the Red Witch. A dull pinkish orb of light appeared above the pieces of her corpse and Ragnar reached out and grabbed it. It solidified into a sphere of otherworldly glass that pulsed with light. Ragnar squeezed the orb and, to Tobin's amazement, the pieces of the Red Witch came back together, like an unseen doctor was stitching her appendages loosely to her torso. When she was whole again she stood on wobbly legs and stared blankly towards Ragnar. She was utterly changed. There was no spark of life left within her, only the hollowness of rotting flesh animated by the wickedest of all the power within the darkness in the Art.

When the bloating and disfigured corpse of the Red Witch walked over to stand beside Ragnar, he turned to face Tobin, cowering behind his rock. Tobin thought Ragnar would repeat the process with him, that he would face the most excruciating death and be brought back to serve Ragnar as a mindless zombie.

"I hope you learned something," said Ragnar before disappearing with the Red Witch in a cloud of black mists.

Tobin stayed there at the mouth of the cave, frozen by fear, until he was found by a search party dispatched by his parents. They had to carry him back to Beddlebern, where he slept for four days straight. When he finally rose he discovered that, in some unexpected way, his plan had worked. His father was attentive and warm while his mother showered him with affection. Their love for their son was no longer shrouded in ambiguity. Only when you think you have lost someone do you realize how important they have been to your happiness. Tobin accepted his parents' sympathetic consolations, trying to forget what had happened, but he could never erase the image of the Red Witch's last living moments from his mind.

A few years later, after Tobin married a suitable Dunmor woman and had two children of his own, news came from the heart of the Atland that troubled him greatly. The Wandering Wizard defeated the Witch-Queen, bringing about an end to her near decade long tyranny but no sooner had she been exiled from the Eternal City than another despot arrived to take her place, this one more fearsome than the last. The tyrant already wore the ancient crown of the Elfin Empresses upon his head and called to him a vast undead army. He, like the Witch-Queen, knew the secret power of necromancy and used it to instill fear into every heart in Albion. He was virtually unopposed as he spread his violence to the four corners of the world.

Where the Witch-Queen had been a woman using the power of the Ring of a Hundred Souls to realize her revenge upon the world, this man was a living god with a sycophantic lust for sadistic fulfillment in the most barbaric and masochistic ways imaginable. Tobin wondered at the identity of this man and was horrified to learn the answer. He was a tall and fearsome looking individual calling himself the Black Prince and he always wore an antique diamond amulet dangling from his neck...

A Wizard and a Witch-Queen

After twenty-three long years of peace under the rule of the Wyt Kings Theron and then Eathon Kalenti, a darkness long dormant in the heart of the Eternal City awoke with a vengeance.

Eathon Kalenti was like his father, Theron, in every way. He was just and kind to both congregants of the Temple of the One God and followers of the Old Religion alike. He was a reasonable man prone to patience but in one thing he had failed greatly: he had become enamored of the Lady Nerys Sanva and insisted she become his wife. Outwardly she appeared to be a virtuous and evocative noblewoman but, in truth, she was a powerful sorceress skilled in working the darkness in the Art. The many years Theron Kalenti ruled as Wyt King, Nerys pretended to be a princess devoted to the Old Religion who doted on her father-in-law. It was only after his death that her true colors began to show. The second she was proclaimed Queen Consort, she began dictating autocratic orders without consulting her husband. She became ruthless and terrifying, bringing the people of Albion to their knees in fear, hoping they would never make the acquaintance of the menacing queen. Eathon, the second Wyt King, tried twice to be rid of her. The first time, he had her kidnapped and smuggled out of the city, taken to the heart of a terrifying forest on the northern slopes of the nearby mountains. The Wyt King was not aware of Nerys' magic and, before her captors had returned to the Eternal City, she was comfortably asleep in her bed.

The second attempt did not bode well for the Wyt King. He resolved he would not just exile Nerys. He would have her quietly assassinated while on the Northern Road, traveling on a royal progress towards the city of Carpathia. It was then the true queen was at last revealed. She obliterated her would-be assassins before transporting herself back to the palace and into the private rooms of the Wyt King. The king was sitting at his desk signing official documents when he noticed his wife appear in the corner, stepping out from the deeps of the shadows. She waltzed over to her husband and stared at him contemptuously, her white beaded gown covered with dirt and her hair severely disheveled.

"I know you sent them, Eathon," she said.

"To what are you referring, dearest one?" asked the Wyt King. Queen Nerys responded by causing the king to choke on his own tongue with the power of the enchanted ring she always wore on her ring finger. The Wyt King gagged and wheezed for nearly a minute, turning as white as a summer cloud, before Nerys released him.

"What did you expect me to do?" sputtered the Wyt King, "you're a monster, Nerys…and everyone knows it."

"I don't care what people think they know," hissed Queen Nerys, "I only care about power, my darling. I married you for power. Now I am killing you for the same reason…"

"It doesn't matter if you murder me today or I die quietly in my sleep years from now," smiled the Wyt King, "I am destined for the Otherworld either way."

"Oh, my dearest," said Nerys, "death by my hand will be far more painful than dying in your bed."

"Do your worst, I'll be dead all the same."

The queen pointed her ring at the Wyt King. At first he seemed unaffected. Then his skin began to change color, growing redder and redder as his eyes bulged from his head. His blood vessels were laid bare as he combusted violently into bright orange flames. When the fire finally burned out, all that remained of the king was a smoldering corpse charred beyond recognition. A small orb of purple light materialized above his remains but, as quickly as it appeared, it began to fade.

"I'm not done with you yet," sneered Nerys. She reached out with her right hand as though she meant to catch the orb like a ball being thrown through the air. The orb returned to its brilliant purple hue and took on a physical texture as Nerys wrapped her long fingers around it. She looked into its depths for a moment, as though it were a crystal ball that would tell her the intricacies of her future. She fondled it for a moment before shoving it into the ruby of her ring, where it disappeared with a soft glow.

"What have you done to me?" said the smoldering remains of the Wyt King.

"I have brought you back from death," smiled Nerys, "I possess such power, you know…the ability to trap a soul and use it to raise the flesh from the grave, to control it, to manipulate it…to make it mine."

"I will never serve you," said the Wyt King.

"Oh, yes you will," laughed Nerys.

Nerys pointed her ring at the smoldering remains of her husband. With a pulse of purple light from the depths of the ruby, the Wyt King went limp, his apprehension melting from his face as he stood and bowed.

"My will is your command, my queen," he said.

Everyone knew what Queen Nerys had done that night but there were none in the Atland with the power to resist her. She openly used her magic against those who spoke out against her and revealed to the world the most devious and terrible of her many powers, the evil craft of necromancy. She had the power to raise corpses from their graves and use them as an undead army to crush any opposition to her usurpation of the crown. The famed Wyt Robes of the Mountain did what they could to counter her magic but the Ring of a Hundred Souls was far too powerful for them to fight.

The Eternal City fell into decay and many parts of Albion broke off into feudal kingdoms warring with one another for regional supremacy. The Witch-Queen didn't care about the outlying lands in Albion. She concentrated her power on the Atland and its surrounding islands. The

Atlandish people were always subdued, held on the brink of death by endless droughts, famines, and plagues. The only land to remain free from the dark influence of the Witch-Queen and her undead army was the tropical island of Ikaria in the rough southern sea, where one of the few Elfkind remaining in Albion used the power of her Autumn Crown to keep the evil of the Witch-Queen at bay.

The Lady Rheis was not the only one possessed of great power dwelling in Ikaria. The Wandering Wizard, Anaximander, had taken up refuge in the Green City of Itheria at the heart of the tropical island. One day he came to the Lady Rheis, troubled by the fate of the world beyond their borders. Anaximander was an aging man using his staff as more of a walking stick than a talisman. He shaved his head in the manner of the Wyt Robes and wore the symbols of the Sacred Masculine and Sacred Feminine tattooed on his scalp. He wore dirty brown robes and a long, wiry beard of the same color, though it had many streaks of white. He was a massive man, easily weighing over 300 pounds and standing as tall as a small bear. He breathed heavily as he approached the throne of the Lady Rheis in her palace at the heart of the Green City.

"I know why you have come, old friend," said the Lady Rheis from where she sat in her natural form, strangely alien yet slightly human. Her skin was the color of milk and her face was distorted by the lack of a nose or lips.

"In the thirty years since I returned from the land beyond the River Lethe I have watched the living world fall into ruin while remaining comfortably here in your kingdom," said Anaximander.

"And now you wish to return to the Atland."

"Yes, my Lady. I must put myself to the purpose of freeing Albion from the Witch-Queen. If I don't than no one will."

"You know the dark source of her magic, the tortured souls trapped within the ring, and not just those of men but those of godly origins as well. It is a power far greater than either of us."

"I am not afraid of the Ring of a Hundred Souls, even if it does hold the spirit of a fallen goddess within its depths."

Anaximander called on the power of the southern winds to carry him upon the clouds to the heart of the Atland. He was aghast at what he saw before him. The once thriving Eternal City, with walls of pure gold and avenues made from rivers of clear blue water, had crumbled into ruin. The golden walls had been stripped and the plaster beneath fallen in many places. There were now dozens of points where one could safely access the city. The blue avenues were black with human waste and rotting corpses for which the Witch-Queen no longer had a use. Anaximander wept for the glorious city lost to memory and was truly moved by the plight of the people he encountered as he made his way slowly towards the Palace of Silver Light at the heart of the city. Their clothes were torn and tattered, their bodies worn and frail. They were unwashed, many with the sores of sickness covering their arms and faces. Dozens approached him on the boardwalk begging for money. Anaximander had no coins to give.

Anaximander's anger mounted as he entered the Palace of Silver Light unopposed. There was not a single guard to be seen. The vast marble hallways were completely abandoned except by overturned statues and grand portraits faded by years of neglect. The windows were shattered, the roof caving in, and the smell of rotting flesh filled the air.

"At last, the Wandering Wizard has come to my doorstep," said a cold voice echoing through the halls.

"I thought it time we should meet," replied Anaximander.

"Then come and join me in the throne room," said the disincarnate voice, *"we will dine on venison and make each other's acquaintance..."*

Anaximander made his way to the great hall at the heart of the palace where he once held an audience with the Last Elfin Empress and had come many times to counsel the first Wyt King. The room was virtually unchanged, although the symbol of the One God had been chipped away from the head of the black throne upon which Nerys was seated. She was dressed in an exquisite gown of green velvet and wore the exotic makeup of the Miri upon her face. On her head sat the Crown of Atlantis while on her ring finger she wore the Ring of a Hundred Souls. As Anaximander slowly approached, Nerys rose from the throne and rushed down the stairs to meet him, a wild grin stretching across her face.

"I can't tell you how long I've wanted to meet you," she said, "I've heard the tales of your many wondrous deeds…you used to advise my father-in-law in the early years of his reign, did you not?"

"I did," replied Anaximander.

"Come…come tell me your stories while we eat," she said, pointing to a small table in the corner of the throne room set with plates of fine china and polished silverware. Anaximander sauntered over to the table and sat down with a sigh of exhaustion.

"Are you not well, Master Anaximander?" asked Nerys, taking the seat opposite him at the table.

"It has been a long journey…"

"I understand. A man of your age traveling so far a distance in so short a time must take its toll. How old are you?"

"Very old."

Three men appeared from a nearby doorway carrying silver trays filled with exotic fruits, nuts, chocolates, dried venison, wine, and water. It took Anaximander only seconds to realize these servants were undead. They had dark bruises around the base of their necks, suggesting they had been strangled or hung. They must have died recently because their decay was minimal. Their skin was even the same color as that of the living.

"I'm sorry, my Lady, but I did not come here to eat," said Anaximander.

"I know why you have come," replied Nerys.

"Then you know what I must do."

"If you must, you must…"

"I am sorry."

"I'm sure you are," replied Nerys.

Anaximander moved faster than one would expect, given his advanced age. He rose from his chair and held his staff before him with both hands, causing a bright sphere of golden light to expand outward around him. The golden light shimmered and sparkled as though it was filled with glitter as a sound like the ringing of a high-pitched bell resonated throughout the air. Anaximander spoke with a voice that boomed like thunder, shaking the foundation of the palace.

"Torvald grym ei twylaeth," he shouted, *"gydarron grym dir leyunara."*

There was a loud crackling sound as the golden sphere charged with purple electricity, pulsing through it like it was the tip of a lightning rod. The electricity grew in intensity and magnificence until it exploded towards Nerys in a shower of cascading light. Nerys didn't budge. She raised her hand and allowed her ring to absorb the electrical assault like a sponge drinking in water. With a flick of her wrist she made the golden sphere surrounding Anaximander implode and, with a wave of her hand, caused the wizard's staff to fly out of his grip and into her waiting arms.

"Tell me, Anaximander, what would happen if I broke this staff in two," asked Nerys, "I would hate for it to kill you."

"Not to worry, it won't, not even your magic is strong enough to touch my soul," said Anaximander.

Like all wizards, Anaximander had long ago removed his soul from his body, placing it within an oaken staff in the manner of the Green Robes. If he were to lose his staff, his powers would be gone, and if Nerys were to succeed in breaking it, he would die. She tried to snap it in two, she hit it with curses and conjured an axe from thin air to chip away at its wooden shell but she was unable to breach the staff or bring harm to Anaximander's soul.

"Damn," smiled Nerys, "we'll have to do this the hard way."

Nerys put her right hand out like she was signaling someone to stop, causing Anaximander to fly through the air. She threw him into the wall again and again until she heard bones begin to snap. She dropped him on his face with such force it knocked out two of his teeth and cracked his cheekbone. She conjured a spear of green flames and bombarded Anaximander with it until his robes and beard had burned away but the green fire did not boil his skin or penetrate his talisman. Slightly confounded, Nerys tried the curse of a thousand deaths but it rebounded, nearly striking her square in the face. She summoned lightning and called the furies. She unsuccessfully conjured a demon and failed in attempting to induce sickness. No matter what she tried, she could not harm Anaximander with her magic.

"Having some trouble?" said Anaximander.

"I may not be able to get to your soul," sneered Nerys, "but I have plenty of others already at my bidding…"

Nerys spoke something in a dark foreign tongue under her breath which ricocheted off the walls as though her voice had been a bullet. Every door leading into the great hall swung open as dozens of undead men rushed through them, answering their mistress' call. They looked at Anaximander with vacant faces, moving slowly towards where he was standing with a bloodlust and a hunger for living flesh. Anaximander stood his ground as the undead moved closer and closer, their faces contorted by hatred.

"*I mi dy ysbryd,*" commanded Anaximander and his staff shook itself free of Nerys' grip, flying through the air back to its master's arms."

"You will not beat me," sneered Nerys.

"*Disgyn yn i'r daiar yn dechaer ei tragwyduil,*" shouted Anaximander.

The earth shook violently, as though a volcano had erupted nearby, releasing chaotic tremors upon the surrounding world. Nerys' eyes narrowed as the shaking grew stronger. One by one, the undead men fell lifelessly to the ground until none remained except for Anaximander and Nerys. Nerys tried to raise them again but her hold over them had been severed.

"I took the liberty of releasing those poor souls from your influence," said Anaximander.

"How dare you!" screamed Nerys. She again lifted Anaximander off the ground and threw him into a wall so hard it crumbled, falling to ruins and burying him in the rubble. She was certain he had met his end. She knew of none who could survive the weight of an entire wall crashing down upon them, least of all a weak old man. She moved to leave the room but, even as she reached the main entrance, there came a deafening boom as the rubble was lifted off the unharmed Anaximander. Nerys sighed, turning back to face the old man again, this time calling forth the most powerful banishing spell she knew, one that would cast his spirit at once from his staff and drive it to the deepest recesses of the void, the place where the spirits of the most malevolent and sadistic beings were condemned forever after death.

"Inoch treax ahazar saphpor atas rahad," she spat. Anaximander was brought to his knees, shaking like he had been charged with an electrical current powerful enough to kill an elephant. Even then he resisted with all his might. He felt his spirit burning to escape his staff, to be ripped from within it by the force of Nerys' spell but he concentrated all his power into keeping himself whole. His nose bled profusely and his eyes nearly swelled shut. He stood weakly, his knees wobbling and his back bent, and smiled despite his many injuries.

"Why won't you die!" wailed Nerys.

"Nerys, you may be the most feared person in the living world because of that ring…you bear the power of hundreds of fallen souls…but I am the emissary of the gods and they are ready to render their judgment."

The roof of the throne room was blown off, as though it had been struck by a powerful gust of wind. The sky was black with heavy storm clouds and rain began to pour down upon them. There were bright flashes of lightning followed by great claps of thunder and the wind howled like the voice of a banshee coming to claim the soul of a fallen man. Then the clouds parted and a bright beam of silver light descended from the heavens, capturing Nerys in its cosmic glow. No harm came to Nerys as she was bathed in the warm light but the Ring of a Hundred Souls slipped from her finger and, with a sound like the shattering of glass, the ruby cracked. It spewed forth soul after soul, culminating in the release of a spirit as black as the moonless night, shrieking in agony from the pain inflicted by the light. The spirits were dragged upwards, passed the broken roof and into the sky, until they disappeared beyond the clouds. The light faded and the storm resumed its onslaught as Nerys fell to the ground.

Nerys shook as her body was inflicted with damage from the loss of the ring. She aged from a beautiful woman in the prime of her life to a hideous old hag with frizzy hair and missing teeth. She looked nothing like the regal woman who brought so much pain to the living world. She was a shell of her former self, like an embarrassing facsimile unsuccessfully passed off as the genuine article. She glared at Anaximander with her nearly blind eyes and spit at him in disgust.

"I'm not beaten yet," she seethed.

"Now you'll have to make your own way in this world," said Anaximander, "without the magic of the ring at your beckoning, you cannot hope to continue your reign of tyranny."

Anaximander bound Nerys in enchanted chains with his staff. The Ring of a Hundred Souls was broken but she still possessed her own spirit and her own formidable power. When they reached the Marshland Forest in the remote outback of the Atland, Anaximander let her free, leaving her on a small mound amidst a foul smelling bog.

"That's it," said Nerys, "you're just going to leave me here? I thought you would kill me."

"You're no longer any threat, except to yourself. If you choose to take your own life from guilt or loneliness it's your business but I will not harm you."

Anaximander left her there in the marshes and Nerys turned towards the dark and dirty water. Nerys laid there beside the smelly bog, unable to gather the strength to stand. She wept, not for her present infirmed state, but for the loss of her position. She had fallen from the most powerful woman in Albion to nothing more than an infirmed old beggar woman in the matter of a single day.

"Mother, mother I need you," she said to no one in particular, "tell me what I must do."

"You must deliver what you promised me," replied an eerie voice, rising from the waters of the bog, *"Bring me three souls…"*

The Sisters and the Well of Shadows

During the first days of the rule of the fearsome Black Prince, as the world was rapidly changing and forgetting the ancient traditions that had governed the Atland for centuries, there lived the four Hanara sisters.

Idris, Aneira, Oryne, and Jadzia, the highborn daughters of the famed Atlandish general, Sir Oran Hanara, were renowned throughout the Atland for their grace and virtue but they were also gullible and unlearned. They were all very beautiful, with almond-shaped eyes the color of honey and long, platinum hair contrasting the rich olive color of their skin. They always wore the finest gowns and jewels and eschewed subtle sexuality. They were devoted to their father and thought he could do no wrong. Sir Oran was a powerful man but he was susceptible to the flaws of men. His daughters had barely reached the age of womanhood when he became very ill, catching the rare and terminal sickness called the Black Sweat.

The sisters did everything they could to save their father's life whom they loved very much, though each held a greater love in the secret places of their heart. Idris, the eldest of the sisters, loved a beautiful ruby necklace given to her by her mother on her deathbed. Aneira, the second eldest, loved a young farmer called Lukat, living in the village near to their father's large estate. Oryne, the third sister, held her prized stallion, Gar, as her greatest possession, while the youngest, Jadzia, loved an old spellbook she had found amidst the ruins of an old tower when she was just a little girl. But their devotion to their various loves was seemingly inferior to the love they held for their father.

In the third week of their father's illness it seemed there was no hope in sight. Idris approached her sisters as they sat outside in the courtyard under the light of the hot afternoon sun. The sisters were identical in appearance. They were often mistaken for quadruplets but Idris possessed a stern and stoic face starting to wrinkle as she approached the last years of her youth.

"Father is getting worse," said Idris, "It's not likely he'll live a week."

"I won't accept it," cried Jadzia, "I can't live without father…"

"What can we do?" asked Oryne, consoling Jadzia by stroking her blonde hair.

"We have to do something," commanded Aneira, "Is there no tonic, no spell that might reverse his decay?"

The sisters were not followers of the Temple of the One God but neither were they devoted to the Old Religion. They loved reading the old legends, speaking of the mythical Elfkind and the unpredictable elemental spirits called the faeries living in a world parallel to Albion. But they were not true believers. Jadzia was the most inquisitive of the sisters. She spent many years studying her spellbook and held a small knowledge of the Art which she used on various occasions to get little things she wanted. Unfortunately, she was no priestess or sorceress. She could think of nothing supernatural that might save their father's life.

"Perhaps we should visit the village apothecary again," said Aneira.

"We have been there six times already," said Idris, "What do you hope to accomplish by doing it again?"

"Perhaps if I apply some pressure on him he will have answers he didn't care to divulge before," said Jadzia, causing her sisters to turn and stare at her with grimaces.

"You mean magic?" asked Oryne, "you know how unpredictable your spells can be. You really want to try using them on the apothecary?"

"I think we should let her try," said Aneira.

"Very well," said Idris defiantly, "we'll visit the apothecary in the morning. But I warn you, Jadzia, do nothing that will cause you harm. Things are bad enough, we don't need to lose you too."

"Alright then," said Aneira, "we will go tomorrow…now go and get some dinner…the afternoon is nearly over."

The following morning the sisters left their home early, walking to the nearby village where the apothecary, Jens Ern, was setting up shop for the day. Jens was a skilled healer and possessed tonics for almost every ailment, except those few terminal illnesses like the Black Sweat. He knew the Atlandish bloodletting rituals. He knew how to cauterize wounds and the craft of setting bones but he was not a practitioner of the Art. He could not conjure a supernatural remedy to cure Sir Oran.

"We wish to speak with you," said Idris as she and her sisters entered the apothecary's shop.

"We don't believe you've been telling us the truth," snapped Oryne, "we know you have a secret cure for our father."

"I'm sorry, m'Ladies, but I don't," said the apothecary.

"We're warning you. We are prepared to force you to tell us," sneered Aneira.

"Forgive me if I'm not overwhelmed by fear," smiled the apothecary.

"Do it, Jadzia," commanded Idris.

Jadzia walked over to stand in front of Jens, pulling a small paring knife from the inside pocket of her cloak. She ran the sharp edge across the face of her right hand, causing bright red blood to pool in her palm. She threw the blood in Jens' face.

"*Caras alieth anarra sanir,*" said Jadzia with a terrifying voice, "*Cathas abreyas talas kir.*"

Jens' eyes lost focus and his face went blank, as though his mind had been wiped and all his desires nullified by the power of Jadzia's spell.

"Now, Jens Ern," said Jadzia, "you will tell me what we wish to know…How do we cure our father?"

"I have no means of curing him here," said the apothecary in a trance, "but I know of someone who might help…she lives in the deep places of the nearby Marshland Forest. You will find her cottage near a withered oak growing in the bogs. That is all I know..."

"*Go to sleep,*" said Jadzia. Jens fell backwards to the floor and began to snore loudly.

"Our path is clear," said Idris, "we must seek out this woman in the swamps."

"I agree," said Oryne.

"As do I," said Aneira.

"Then let's go find her," said Jadzia.

The sisters set out straightaway for the Marshland Forest a few miles from the village. The road was treacherous. A few times, the sisters fell into the marshes and were nearly drowned by the weeds and underwater brambles. By the time the moon began to rise in the night sky they had arrived at a large bog where a withered old oak was growing next to a small rickety cottage with smoke rising from its stonework chimney. The sisters hadn't come any closer to the little house when an old black raven flew down from the sky and perched itself on the dead branches of a nearby tree.

"What brings four such lovely young ladies into the heart of the swamp?" cawed the raven, blinking its beady little eyes.

"We seek the woman who lives in this cottage," said Oryne, "we need her help with an urgent matter."

"You have not come here in violence?" asked the raven.

"We need a remedy for our father," said Idris.

"If that is all you seek then I may be able to help you..."

Suddenly the raven jumped down from the tree branch it had been perched on and landed at the sisters' feet, twisting and growing and shedding its feathers until an elderly woman clothed all in rags stood where the bird had been. She was bent and withered, holding a cane fashioned in the image of a snake and shaking constantly from the damage time had done to her nervous system. She extended a hand, inviting the sisters to join her inside the cottage, consisting of a single room with a large hearth with an old table and chairs sitting next to the fire, a feather bed in the corner, and a piss pot near the front door.

"Can you help us?" asked Aneira.

"I cannot cure your father," said the old woman, "but I may know a way you can heal him yourselves."

"How?" asked Idris.

"Not far from here in the deepest places of these very woods stands the legendary Well of Shadows...I'm sure you've heard of it."

None of the sisters answered. They had never heard of such a thing, not in legend nor in scripture.

"The waters within the well have the power to grant a single wish but I warn you now, this gift comes with a price...you must offer whatever you love most to the Nameless Goddess, guardian of the well, by dropping it into her waters. Only then will she bless you with her magic..."

"And if we don't give the well our dearest love?" asked Jadzia.

"The Nameless Goddess will claim your souls as payment for your deception," replied the old woman.

"That sounds far too dangerous," replied Idris, "I will not allow my sisters to take such a risk."

"Unfortunately for you, my dears, the spell will take at least three of you to accomplish...to bring someone back from the brink of death is no easy feat. Think hard before you decide to take this course of action and ask yourselves if your father's life is worth it."

"I say we do it," said Jadzia, ready and willing to sacrifice anything to save her father.

"Yes, no price is too great for father," said Oryne less convincingly.

"I agree," muttered Aneira.

"Then I guess we're going to the Well of Shadows," said Idris quietly, "How do we find it?"

"I will enchant a compass to show you the way," said the old woman. She produced a small copper compass from inside a cabinet near where she was seated. She waved her hand over it while muttering something under her breath and it momentarily lit up with golden light. The old woman handed the compass to Idris before grabbing her gently by the wrist.

"Be careful, child," she said, "go now and gather your most beloved things. Only they possess the power to appease the Nameless Goddess."

The sisters returned to their home near the spring village and slept warily until the sun's first light. Jadzia had already produced her spellbook and was waiting by the door when the other three sisters appeared from their rooms, groggy from a lack of sleep.

"Hurry sisters," said Jadzia, "father is growing weaker."

"We will need time to gather our beloved things," said Oryne, "let's meet back here in two hours. Then we will set out for the well."

Idris went to her room to retrieve the ruby necklace given to her by her mother but, as she looked upon its beauty, she decided she could not part with it. Instead, she chose to take her pearl-handled comb because it too was dear to her heart, though not to the same degree as the necklace. Aneira went to the nearby village to convince her lover to accompany them to the well so that she might push him in but, as she gazed into his warm blue eyes, she knew she could never be apart from him. She returned to her home and retrieved the parakeet she had kept as a pet since she was a child. Finally, Oryne didn't even feign a desire to sacrifice her stallion. She decided to offer up her favorite pair of shoes. The three older sisters were convinced that the love they felt for these objects would be enough to save their father.

The sisters were devoted to their father but they fostered within their hearts vain ambitions and selfish thoughts. They were conceited and compared their beauty to that of the Old Goddesses and gloated about their position and prestige. Their father only helped to cement those feelings, spoiling each daughter rotten and refusing to allow them to marry. His own wife had died several years earlier and the sisters reminded him of her greatest qualities. In those moments after their father got sick, the sisters felt they must save him to repay him all his kindnesses.

The journey to the Well of Shadows took nearly a day. The sisters traversed rugged, swampy territory which they were entirely unfamiliar with. The light of the sun was blocked by the eves of the ancient trees growing amidst the reedy bogs. The sisters grew fearful as they rushed through the woods. Luckily, the enchanted compass never failed them. It showed them all the safe paths through the marsh, taking them to a small island at the heart of the forest. On the little island stood the ruined foundation of a tower, long since destroyed by the decays of time, and an old stone well. The sisters tiptoed to the edge of the well and peered into its depths. The water within had a strangely black hue, like the surrounding light was being drawn into its depths rather than reflected from its surface.

"Who comes to stand before my waters?" said a mysterious voice echoing out from the deeps of the well. The water began to ripple and churn before rising up and forming the silhouette of a woman, tall and proud, dressed in flowing robes of silver.

"We are the Hanara Sisters from the Kalra Province," said Idris, "we have come to wish our father returned to good health…"

"And you are willing to offer me the things you love the most as payment for this wish?" said the Nameless Goddess.

Each sister stepped forward and dropped the object they had brought with them into the well: Idris offered her comb, Aneira her parakeet, Oryne her shoes, and Jadzia her spellbooks. The waters of the well were lit up with an eerie gray glow expelled from the depths like light escaping a lantern. Then the glow sputtered out with a crackle and returned the island to darkness. The sisters looked at one another, shaking with fear.

"Shame on you, Sisters Hanara," spat the Nameless Goddess, *"all but one have tried to deceive me. Payment must be rendered as the price of your lies."*

Idris, Oryne, and Aneira began to twitch with pain, like someone had lit up their nervous system with microscopic fire. A dark purple light materialized around them, growing brighter and brighter until there came a blinding silver flash. The three older sisters screamed. When the light faded, three small purple orbs were revolving in the air around the watery silhouette. The three older sisters were pulling themselves weakly off the ground and looked haggard and frail, as though they had aged ten years in a single minute. Jadzia's spellbook was lying on the ground near the edge of the well with the comb, the parakeet, and the ornate pair of shoes. All were soaked but no worse for wear.

"These things I return to you," said the Nameless Goddess, *"but your souls I shall keep forever in the deep places of my well. One day, when death comes for you, you shall again see my face, Sisters Three. Until then…"*

The sisters gathered their belongings and returned home in shame. Jadzia berated her older sisters the entire journey for their inability to sacrifice their beloved treasures to save their father's life. When they arrived at their estate they were greeted by Jens Ern who told them the sad news. Their father had quietly passed away alone, without his daughters there to comfort and soothe him in his final minutes. The sisters were devastated. Idris retired to her room and refused to see anyone for nearly a month. Aneira moved off the estate and openly declared her love for Lukat, taking up his bed every night as his wife and companion. Oryne barely spoke, spending her days sitting in the library with the blinds pulled shut, crying in the darkness. Jadzia poured over her spellbook, looking for something she may have missed, but she found nothing that would bring their father back.

Sadly, the devastation had only just begun. Only eleven days after putting their father to rest in the family tomb, Oryne was struck down by a mysterious cough, slowly filling her lungs with fluid until she choked to death on her own mucus. Two weeks later, Aneira was murdered by Lukat in a jealous rage after seeing her flirting with a neighbor. Then Idris began to complain of pains in her stomach and took to her bed. Jadzia tended to her sister's needs. She brought her broth and warm milk every day and washed her nightly with a sponge.

"Oh, sister," said Idris weakly, "I fear I will soon join our sisters in the grip of that Nameless Goddess of the Well. We should never have gone there, Jadzia. We should never have risked so much."

"No, Idris. You and Aneira and Oryne should never have lied," said Jadzia, "you knew what the cost would be and still you did it. Why?"

But Idris gave no answer. Her final words had also carried with them her last breath as she laid there with eyes staring blankly at Jadzia. Jadzia cried as the servants came to carry Idris away, to be interred alongside Aneira and Oryne. Jadzia wept for her sister, whom she had loved, but also for her own loneliness and despair. She lost the last of her love as she attended the funerary rites and contempt crept slowly into her mind as she plotted for a way to be reunited with the ones she loved.

After many months had passed and Jadzia had grown bitter and mad, she decided to take her prized spellbook and again visit the Well of Shadows.

"You have returned," said the Nameless Goddess, rising from the well, *"What do you seek now?"*

"I want my sisters back," said Jadzia, "if only for a day or even an hour…I cannot live without seeing their faces again."

"What you ask is not possible. Their souls are in my keeping and I will not give them up…"

"Then return me their bodies," said Jadzia weakly, "they lived for many months without their souls…I'm sure they can live again."

"They did not live long without their souls…the soul is what animates the body. Without it one cannot hope to survive. Only wizards and gods know the secret of surviving without their soul inside them…but even they keep them close. If your soul is lost then you are lost…there is no coming back."

"I will seek out a god or a wizard to learn this secret."

"The gods no longer dwell in Albion and the Wizarding Clans would never divulge such a secret to a commoner with only a modicum of comprehension when it comes to the Art. Many wizards have died to protect that secret."

"Then there is no way," said Jadzia.

"There is always a way," laughed the Nameless Goddess, *"it is merely that the power to reanimate the dead without the presence of their soul is beyond me."*

"I have decided upon my wish," said Jadzia before throwing her spellbook into the well, "I wish to be forever young."

The well belched forth a powerful green light that blinded Jadzia as the air was filled with a deafening sound like millions of birds taking wing from the surrounding trees. The sky was blackened and the wind began to howl. Strange noises filtered through the water, terrifying Jadzia as she stood there in amazement. As the light faded Jadzia saw her hands were those of a teenager, her breasts were firm, and her body slim and taut. Her hair was long and flowing while her skin was smooth and soft. She had indeed been blessed with the gift of eternal youth.

"Why did you decide upon immortality?" asked the Nameless Goddess as she shrank back into the well.

"You do not know of a way for me to bring my sisters back but it might be possible," said Jadzia, "I intend to search the four corners of the world for as long as it takes until I find the answer...I will have my sisters back and then, then we will come for you."

Jadzia turned on her heel and waltzed away from the well. The Nameless Goddess faded back into the dark waters in its depths, believing one day Jadzia's prophecy would come to pass. Jadzia would find a way to reanimate her sisters and they would come for her in the dark of the night to retrieve the souls she stole from them. The Nameless Goddess had inadvertently used her own godly magic to create a formidable new enemy.

Jadzia kept her word and began searching for the means to realize her revenge against the Nameless Goddess. She returned to the cottage of the Swamp Witch with the intention to bully the old hag into helping her but she found the rickety old house abandoned. She searched and searched. She found no trace of the woman who sent her and her sisters to the Well of Shadows. On her tirade, Jadzia stumbled into the court of the Black Prince but that is another story…

From the Darkness

When the spirit of the Nameless Goddess reached the Palace of the Dead on the far edge of the Otherworld, she was weak but full of hatred. She fell upon the floor before the thrones of the Old Gods, who were weakened by the great magic that broke the Ring of a Hundred Souls and brought an end to the Witch-Queen's nine years of tyranny. It is the nature of the gods to remake for themselves bodies of flesh when their spirit is free to do so but the Nameless Goddess was restrained by the power of the gods who feared she might gather her strength and bring war to the Otherworld.

"We meet again," said Maru, goddess of the waxing moon.

"Not by my will," hissed the Nameless Goddess.

"We cannot judge you for the evil wrought by the Witch-Queen," said Annatar, god of fire, "you were a prisoner within the ring, but neither can we ignore it was by your will she began her journey into the darkness. If we believed in killing our own kind, as you have done, we would put you quickly to death and bring an end to your wretched soul. But we do not kill...therefore we will banish you back to the Well of Shadows from whence you came in the hopes that you will finally see the error of your ways and one day beg us for pardon."

"Your earthy body is still made from those impure waters," said Narenna, goddess of the waning moon, "we simply mean to rejoin your two halves...it is what must be done to restore the balance..."

The gods and goddesses acted in synchronicity, drawing a great white light down upon the Nameless Goddess who was at once transported back to the dark waters of the well at the heart of the marshland forest. She was rejoined to her body and her consciousness made whole but she was trapped as she had been when she was cast out of the Otherworld for killing the One God. She had known only a brief moment of freedom, when Nerys sacrificed the virtue of a warrior man to allow her to remake her flesh. But she had been betrayed, her body once again becoming that blackwater in the darkness, deprived of its spirit, trapped within the Ring of a Hundred Souls. From that moment on the Nameless Goddess was living two lives from two opposing perspectives. She was both in the well and in the ring and could see events transpiring from each. If someone had come to seek her out in the well, she would've appeared to them as a watery apparition but if one had called to her in the ring she would also have responded. It wasn't until her spirit had been returned to her body in the well that she could again form thoughts and bring a focus to her anger.

After the Witch-Queen had been deposed by the Old Gods and their emissary, Anaximander, the power of the darkness began to wane. The Nameless Goddess felt herself weaken but still had the strength to hear Nerys calling to her from afar.

"Mother, mother help me," called Nerys, "Tell me what I must do to become strong again…"

"Bring me the three souls you promised," replied the Nameless Goddess, overwhelmed by a desire to live again. She no longer needed the three souls to revive herself in body and spirit. She had another idea for their uses. She knew of a Red Tower on the edge of the Wynterlande Forest where an elfin sorceress called the Red Witch dwelt. Within its walls was hidden the Amulet of the One God and the Nameless Goddess meant to use the power of the three fallen spirits to acquire it and make it her own. She would sacrifice the souls in an ancient spell that would not only free her from the Well of Shadows and remake her body, but also give her the power to take the amulet as her own.

As luck would have it, there came four vain sisters to the Well of Shadows seeking the power to save the life of their father. They were sent by

Nerys, who had begun calling herself the Swamp Witch. The Nameless Goddess asked each sister to sacrifice their most beloved possession, knowing that they would never acquiesce to her price...the penalty being the forfeiture of their souls. Not three souls but four. The Nameless Goddess underestimated the youngest sister, Jadzia, who indeed gave her most sacred possession to save her father. The spell was not fulfilled because the other sisters lied, their souls passing into the keeping of the Nameless Goddess. The fourth sister eventually returned and again gave the Nameless Goddess what she asked of for. The Nameless Goddess was forced by the laws of magic to bless her with immortality, knowing one day she would return and demand the return of her sisters' souls.

The Nameless Goddess had failed to see the return of her hated enemy, the Black Prince, who reclaimed the Amulet of the One God and used its awesome power to conquer Atlantis after the fall of the Witch-Queen. He raised an undead army larger than that of Queen Nerys and used it to impose his will upon the world. With the amulet in his possession, the Nameless Goddess could see no way to defeat him and claim power for herself. The Ring of a Hundred Souls was gone and the Autumn Crown was in the possession of the Lady of the Green City. There were no other godly talismans left with the power needed to resurrect herself so the three souls stolen from the sisters remained resting with the Nameless Goddess at the bottom of her well.

Jadzia, who had been made immortal by the power of the Nameless Goddess, began learning in earnest all the parts of the darkness in the Art and saw the Black Prince as a way to acquire the means to restore her sisters to life. She approached him while he sat on the throne of the Wyt Kings in the Eternal City, trembling in fear at the awesomeness of his giant and fearsome presence. She bowed before his terrifying majesty with great effort not to look him directly in the eyes.

"I must have my sisters returned to me," she pleaded.

"And you would pay any price?" asked the Black Prince.

"Any," replied Jadzia.

"If you promise to serve me always as my lieutenant and consort, then I will go now to the Well of Shadows and free your sisters' spirits from the clutches of that evil nameless lady."

"I will serve you always…I swear."

"Be prepared, child, I might succeed in retrieving your sisters' spirits but I cannot reunite them with their bodies."

"I don't understand."

"To resurrect the living is an impossible task," said the Black Prince, "the flesh may be raised from the grave if one possesses mastery over the soul once housed in that body but, if the soul is placed again within the flesh, it will move on to the Otherworld, as all souls must when their time comes to die…"

"Then my sisters are lost to me forever," cried Jadzia.

"Not entirely…if you still mean to serve me I will give their souls to you and you may do what you wish with them…you can raise their flesh from the ground so they walk here with you again in the living world, you can use them to create a powerful talisman that would set you higher than any other mortal witch, or you can allow them to pass quietly into the Otherworld…it is your choice but whatever you decide you will always be my servant. Agreed?"

"Agreed."

The Black Prince left that night, moving through the darkness like a vampire looking for its evening meal. He arrived at the Well of Shadows in the early hours of the morning and called the Nameless Goddess to stand before him as the watery apparition she had become so long ago. She looked upon the Black Prince with contempt as he returned her gaze with hatred boiling out from the dark brown of his evil eyes.

"Why have you come here, Ragnar?" she asked.

"I have come for the souls of the Sisters Hanara," replied the Black Prince, "and I will take them by force if necessary…"

"It won't need to come to that," said the Nameless Goddess, "I'm sure we can come to some kind of agreement…it was after all your authority that condemned me to this watery grave and it would be only fitting for you to free me…if you allow me to reclaim my body and walk again under the light of the moon, I will gladly give you the three souls in my keeping."

"Why would I ever allow you your freedom?" grinned the Black Prince, "You are the most dangerous enemy I have ever known…to let you free would be to sign my own death warrant…"

"Oh please," replied the Nameless Goddess, "you know I haven't the power to face you alone…if I had the Autumn Crown or the Ring of a Hundred Souls it would be different but both are beyond my reach…you have the Amulet of the One God, the jewel of my own making. Its power is no longer mine to command…I simply wish to be free to worship under the light of the moon and live my life again"

The Black Prince watched the Nameless Goddess for several minutes before he made his decision. With the power of the Amulet of the One God, he enveloped the Nameless Goddess' watery visage in silvery light. With the passing of each second each part of her took on a fleshy substance until she stood body and soul upon the ground, naked and shivering with her raven black hair wild and unkempt. She looked deviously at the Black Prince, like he was something revolting stuck to the bottom of her shoe before she retrieved the three souls in her keeping from the bottom of the well, handing them to the Black Prince like precious marbles being passed from one collector to the next.

"Never cross me, Tsira," said the Black Prince menacingly.

"I wouldn't dare," smiled the Nameless Goddess, bowing slightly to show her respect.

"See that you don't," replied the Black Prince.

The Black Prince then returned to the Palace of Silver Light at the heart of the Eternal City and called Jadzia to him, giving into her keeping the three souls of her sisters.

"Was it difficult to defeat the Nameless Lady?" asked Jadzia.

"I did not defeat her," replied the Black Prince.

"Then how?"

"We struck a deal...the souls of your sisters for her freedom."

"You set her free?" asked Jadzia angrily, "that wasn't part of our deal..."

"It is now," said the Black Prince fiercely, "and you would do well to remember to whom you are speaking..."

Jadzia retreated from the Eternal City that night, journeying to the ancestral tomb of her forefathers and lighting candles upon the altar of the God of Death to pray for guidance. She had never been an evil woman. In fact, she had been the purest of all the Hanara sisters but time had brought her to the edge of darkness. She now hungered for power. She was on the brink of performing the ritual to join the spirits of her sisters with their bodies so that they might pass to the Otherworld peacefully when she was reminded she would afterwards be forever alone. Instead, she spilt her own blood upon the altar and spoke a terrible enchantment, frothing from her mouth like poison.

"Meirwon Idris, Meirwon Oryne, Meirwon Aneira," she said.

With sounds like rats scurrying across wooden floorboards, the corpses of the three Hanara sisters took a raspy breath. Each sat up upon their funeral slab, their place of eternal slumber and looked at one another in horror. They had been gone only a few short years but the decays of time were evident in their putrefied gray skin. They stunk of rotting flesh and looked haggard and withered. Their extremely long hair had turned white and frail while their teeth were gone altogether. They were rotting away more each day and knew they were still dead. They stood weakly, looking for the source of their awakening. When they spotted Jadzia they sauntered over to her with eerie, vacant faces.

"Explain this sister," said Idris with the voice of a corpse.

"I brought you back," replied Jadzia.

"Why would you do such a thing?" said Oryne, "we were at peace."

"Because...I've been so lonely. I need you, sisters..."

"You were always selfish, Jadzia, selfish and ignorant," said Aneira, "we are dead and your spell will not change that...as you continue to live, we will continue to rot until nothing remains but hollow bones."

"Send us back," yelled Idris, "put us back in our eternal sleep...please."

"I can't," cried Jadzia, "I need you..."

"Put us back," yelled Oryne. Together with the other two undead sisters she advanced on Jadzia, as though they meant to strangle the life from her for her insolence.

"STOP," screamed Jadzia. Each sister stepped back, dropping her arms to her sides.

"Your wish is our command, mistress," they said in unison.

"That's better," said Jadzia.

The dead Hanara sisters followed Jadzia back to her chambers where they wrapped themselves in crimson shrouds, hiding their decaying flesh and adding a fearsome mystique to their already imposing presence. From that day forward, they became the Shadow-Weavers, the greatest servants of the Black Prince. The Black Prince may have known from the beginning what Jadzia would do but he said nothing. He quietly waited for her to resurrect her sisters and fall fully into the darkness so that he might manipulate her to the fullest extent...

The Other Side

Nerys died alone in her bed with no one to mourn her. She spent the last years of her life living in seclusion amongst the reeds and twisted trees of a remote marshland, her only visitor being the Wandering Wizard, Anaximander, who would bring her dried meats and fresh vegetables before sitting down to tea and cakes and discussing the comings and goings in the outside world. At one time, Anaximander had been Nerys' most fearsome enemy but, after she had been stripped of her enchanted ring, he showed her pity and kindness. She was once the most powerful woman in the living world but those days were in the past, mere memories fading from her geriatric mind as she slowly met her end in the dank of her crumbling cottage.

Nerys took to her bed in the coldest days of winter and did not rise again. She developed a terrible cough which stole her breath and caused her limbs to go numb. She felt her strength leaving her and she lost her ability to work magic, to even understand the intricacies of the Art. She shivered constantly despite covering herself with several blankets and she always slept restlessly. Finally, she exhaled a raspy breath, allowing her jaw to drop and her heart to stop. For a few moments everything went dark before Nerys opened her eyes. She was no longer lying under her blankets in her marshland cottage. She was standing in the middle of a wide green field under the light of the bright summer sun, a wide river flowing by in the distance. She thought for a moment that she was hallucinating because she was standing there as flesh and blood before remembering that, when we die, our spirits take on the same substance they knew in life as they pass into the Otherworld. But she had not come to the Otherworld yet. She was in the place between the mists and the River Lethe, existing as neither the living world nor the land of the dead but as a gateway connecting both, called Avalon by the ancients, the Blessed Isles where travel the souls of the dead.

Avalon was once the home of the faerie folk but they had long ago disappeared, leaving no traces of their civilization beyond the mists. Nerys had heard the stories of the only other mortal besides Anaximander to pass safely through the mists, a young man called Norvo, from the Easterling Tribes beyond the Deepening Ocean. Norvo never returned from the shores of Avalon but it was said that he fell in love with a Faerie Princeling and together they crossed into the Otherworld, never to be seen again. The story did nothing to explain the disappearance of the faeries but, shortly thereafter, the Elfin Empress forbid mortal men from learning the secret ways through the mists. The faeries and Elfkind were allies and closely related by blood but the faeries were more in tune with the natural elements while the Elfkind bore greater wisdom when practicing the Art. The faerie folk had always dwelt in Avalon, making their sudden disappearance even more of a mystery. Nerys would've gladly roamed those hills between the worlds in search of the lost faerie civilization because it was believed that of all the races in all the realms, the faeries were the only beings who knew the secret of raising someone from the dead, not only as a corpse, but as a living, breathing person with their soul intact. The thought of returning to the living world to start her life again thrilled Nerys but that jubilation was quickly overcome by the reality that the magic of the faeries had mysteriously vanished right alongside them.

Nerys was suddenly struck by a fear of the unknown. The only living man to pass into the Otherworld and return unscathed was Anaximander and he never spoke of his secret adventures beyond the River Lethe. The Elfkind had also been skilled in traveling unharmed between the worlds but, like the Wandering Wizard, they never spoke of their dealings with the Old Gods. She sat down upon the soft, unkempt bluegrass and began to sob, gently laying her head in her lap. She had never been able to admit her fears but she came close in that hour.

"It's time," said a familiar voice as Nerys looked up to see Anaximander standing over her, his bald head reflecting the light of the sun, his wiry beard as dirty and unkempt as his dingy brown robes.

"What? Are you dead too?" asked Nerys.

"No, no, of course not," replied Anaximander, "I am the Master of the Mists. I have free license to travel between the worlds without consequence whenever I choose. I am no stranger to these lands…"

"And you've come to be sure that I'm dead," sneered Nerys.

"I have come to join you on your journey," said Anaximander, "it may be a difficult road ahead…I did not want you to face it alone…"

"You should hate me…"

"I don't hate."

Anaximander took Nerys by the hand and together they walked away towards the river in the distance. Before they arrived at the shore Anaximander slipped a gold coin into Nerys' hand as payment for the Ferryman. Near an old decaying dock with a small barge tied to it they came upon an emaciated and gangly Ferryman wrapped in a black cloak. Anaximander placed a gold coin in his hand and signaled for Nerys to do the same before they boarded the barge. Anaximander sat with Nerys at the front while the cloaked man poled the craft across the river.

The River Lethe was an ancient boundary that sang with the power of the universe, charged with the voice of its creator. The water bore a perfect silver hue and seemed to be undisturbed by the Ferryman's pole as they glided towards the center of the river. The current was so strong it seemed the tiny barge would be dragged downstream and away from the shores of the Otherworld, leading Nerys to wonder what existed down the river. Did it just fall off the edge of the world like a waterfall flowing into the nothingness of space or did it lead to yet another fantastic realm unexplored by man? Judging by his face, she was sure Anaximander knew the answer but he was not going to reveal it to her under any circumstances.

As Nerys peered into the still water she began to see faces staring back at her from the deeps, cold and lifeless images of souls trapped beneath the surface, doomed to remain a part of that mystic river.

"Who are they?" Nerys quietly asked Anaximander as they continued to move across the calm river.

"They are the souls of those sad few denied entrance to the Otherworld because of their desire to punish themselves for their deeds in life," said Anaximander.

"Can they ever be freed?"

"If that is what they choose."

"I don't understand…"

"Those poor spirits are doomed to the deeps of the river by their own choice," replied Anaximander, "because they are not willing to forget the woes of their lives. If they are willing to forgive themselves, they will be released."

When they arrived upon the distant shore, the cloaked man grounded the barge on a sandy beach so that Anaximander and Nerys could disembark without wading through the treacherous shallows of the river. A few yards off they came to a road of silver stones leading towards rolling hills covered in grass off in the distance. They took up the path and were quickly underway.

Nerys stopped at the edge of the path, again overwhelmed by fear, but Anaximander urged her onward. It took far less time than it should have for them to reach those distant hills and, before the sun had set that evening, they were on the other side, in a narrow valley surrounded by snowcapped mountains. They never encountered a single creature, not an animal, not a roaming spirit, not even a bird perched leisurely in a tree. As the twilight set in, they settled at the edge of a small brook at the heart of the valley for the night. Anaximander built a fire for warmth but it never truly grew dark. The sky remained gray with a dull silver light as the full moon rose brightly into the heavens. The Otherworld was free from the menace of darkness.

"Tell me something, Anaximander," said Nerys, "Will I suffer?"

"I don't understand the question," replied Anaximander, "What do you mean by suffer?"

"I mean, will the gods punish me for my crimes? For serving the Nameless Goddess?"

"The only punishment you will find here is the one you impose upon yourself," replied Anaximander.

"I don't understand."

"You will…"

As the sun rose the next morning they resumed their journey towards the heart of the Otherworld. They traveled over a narrow pass through the mountains and at last came to a wide highland plane overlooking a vast ocean of purple water. There were two cities in the distance, one with towers of silver, the other with palaces of gold. Beyond them, upon a tall mountain at the edge of the sea, stood an enormous palace of ivory with crystal terraces and towers of jade ringed by downy white clouds. The sky was a bright shade of blue and the air was filled with the smell of wildflowers as the pair trekked down towards the cities in the distance, slowly walking along the road of silver stones and taking in the beauty of the scenery.

"The City of Gold is called Elnurea," said Anaximander, "it's the destination of all souls of men after they take their final breath and depart the living world."

"And the City of Silver?" asked Nerys.

"It is called Elmaeth," replied Anaximander, "it is where the spirits of the Elfkind gather to live in communion with one another."

"And beyond is the Palace of the Dead," said Nerys. She knew enough of the Mysteries to recognize the home of the old gods.

"Yes, but the spirits of the dead do not venture there…"

"Am I not meant to stand before the gods to atone for my earthly sins? Is that not what the Old Religion teaches us?"

"As I told you already, you will find no one who will judge you here…and the gods have more on their minds than the trivial pursuits of one misguided and selfish woman."

Anaximander's words stung Nerys, not because she believed herself above his insults but because she had always thought of herself in greater terms. She had conquered the whole of the living world, commanding armies of undead warriors and bringing the fear of her name to every home across Albion. Yet here in the Otherworld she was only a selfish woman. She stopped there upon the road as the Witch-Queen reemerged from the deeps of Nerys' consciousness where she had been sleeping for years.

"You dare to compare me to other women?" she said harshly.

"I would counsel you to control your temper here, Nerys," said Anaximander forcefully, "Dark shadows cannot remain in this realm without paying a great price…that is the only rule of the Otherworld."

Nerys felt her anger well up within her like hot water boiling over the edge of a pot. She glared at Anaximander with complete indifference, as though she had heard nothing he had just said. All her hatred from the years of her miserable life exploded out of her mouth as she cursed the Otherworld and the Old Gods and Anaximander. Her curses were so hateful that they became tangible, forming a giant ball of green fire hovering over Nerys' head but, as soon as the flames flickered into life, there came a loud wailing from above their heads and Nerys looked up to see a ghostly figure swooping down from the sky above her, screaming so fiercely that her ears began to burn.

"What is that?" said Nerys, dropping the green fire to the ground.

"A banshee," replied Anaximander.

"What does it want?"

"You…"

"But you said I would find no judgment here."

"I told you that you would create your own punishment, and this is it," said Anaximander.

The banshee flew down and grabbed Nerys by the shoulders with its razor talons, yanking her upward like a mouse caught by a hungry eagle, carried away into the lofty reaches of the summer sky. They kept flying up and up and up until they breached the sphere of the Otherworld and entered the darkness of space. Suddenly the stars ceased to shine and the air around them warped and twisted like an oil painting doused with turpentine. The banshee screamed again before releasing Nerys from its grip. She fell through the rapidly disintegrating darkness. She thought she would float there forever amidst the nothingness and was surprised when she splashed down into an unseen body of water. The currents carried her deeper and deeper despite her best efforts to swim to the surface. It seemed like she was wrapped in an invisible chain, its weight pulling her to the bottom. She felt herself be transmuted as her fleshy exterior faded, replaced by the same watery substance in which she was being held prisoner.

"I warned you about violence in the Otherworld, Nerys, and now here we are," said Anaximander as he appeared before her, not in the flesh but as a ghostly and translucent phantom.

"And where is here?" asked Nerys.

"You are still within the Land of the Dead," replied Anaximander, "but you have been condemned to the River Lethe, the place where spirits who wish to punish themselves are sent to work out their fears…"

"I am not afraid."

"You have always been afraid, Nerys…ever since you were a little girl you feared unhappiness so much that you were determined at all costs to make others love you…but your parents never did and you despised them for it…and for marrying you to Dernevariost when you were only sixteen. The greatest hardship you had to endure was the loss of your love, Gyrdhan and your fear to love again drove your hatred, your bitter need for revenge, until you had become more of a monster than anyone who ever wronged you. And here you are, still unwilling to let go of your hatred and your fear…"

"I don't know how," admitted Nerys.

"You will remain here until you learn," said Anaximander before his phantom faded like a sandcastle washed away by a violent wave.

"You haven't seen the last of me, wizard," she shouted.

Nerys remained there in the depths of the River of the Dead for an untold span of years, never once considering forgiveness as an option. Her hatred burned too hot to ever be extinguished by the cooling waters of the river. Instead she concentrated her rage on her deep prison, hoping to ignite another burst of magic like the green ball of fire. It seemed that her efforts were ineffective as she continued to fade into the current, becoming one with the other lost souls doomed to share her fate and be forgotten by the world beyond the river.

"I will find a way," she exclaimed to herself.

Suddenly a great swirling whip of green fire erupted from Nerys' fading spirit, cutting a path through her watery prison. She emerged on the Avalon side of the River. The moment she caught light of the sun her flesh was reconstituted so that, even though she was dead, she stood there like a living woman. The great hilly expanse was still absent any signs of life but Nerys was determined to discover what had become of the faeries, desiring above all else a way to return to Albion and live again. She would not stop until she found a way.

Nerys searched from the wall of mists to the water's edge, from a great hedge maze to a wide impassible ravine but she found no clues that would set her on the path to finding the faeries. Then, upon her sixth day of looking, she stumbled across a strange monolith marked with unreadable runes, decaying as though it had stood for millennia. She wondered why this monolith would remain when all else had disappeared and placed her hands upon it, feeling the runes with her fingers. No sooner had she finished tracing the bizarre markings than there came a bright white glow, as though a curtain had fallen to reveal an earthbound sun shining with the light of a thousand stars. Nerys covered her eyes to protect herself from the glare as she noticed the vague silhouette of a shadowy figure strolling out from the heart of the light.

The silhouette took a ghostly form, revealing a tall figure with long hair the color of molten silver and cat-like eyes of a deep violet. He was naked, his perfectly shaped body and elongated limbs absent any markings or hair. He had two rings of light protruding from his back, like the wings of a butterfly had been grafted to his flesh and lit up with sparklers. He looked curiously at Nerys before speaking.

"Who are you?" he asked.

"I am Queen Nerys," she replied regally, "Mistress of the Darkmoon, Protector of the Shadows, and Sovereign of the Living World."

"At last! We've had such a need!"

"A need for what?"

"A queen," smiled the faerie man.

Faceless

After the battle that deposed the Black Prince, exiling him forever into the void, the Wyt Robes became the Stewards of Atlantis in the name of the Old Religion. Meanwhile, their enemies, the Grey Robes, plotted in the darkness, seeking to retake control of Albion. The Ruined City of Tansapar became the heart of evil in the living world as the Grey Robes and their allies gathered to conspire and scheme. Once a thriving metropolis, rich with gold and mercantile treasures, Tansapar was the last stronghold of the rebels resisting the authority of the Black Prince. Demonstrating the extent of his power, the Black Prince ripped the walls down with his bare hands before calling terrifying demons from the darkness to destroy his enemies with untold brutality. Afterwards the city was claimed as an outpost by the greatest of the Grey Robes under the prince's authority.

"We must act quickly brothers, before the Wyt Robes have a chance to consolidate their authority over the Eternal City," said Gareth, a highly skilled practitioner of the darkness in the Art and leader of the Grey Robes. The other members of his brotherhood were scattered throughout the main hall of the crumbling Summer Palace listening intently.

"If the Black Prince didn't have the power to stand against the Wyts, how do you expect us to fare any better?" said a man from the crowd.

"We will find a way, brothers," replied Gareth.

Gareth couldn't think of a single course of action that would ensure victory against the Wyt Robes. The Black Prince was a living god with the Amulet of the One God in his possession and he had been defeated by the magic of the Wyts. There were no more talismans forged by the hands of the Old Gods left in Albion, except for the Autumn Crown, resting firmly upon the head of the Elfin Lady of the Green City, completely beyond the reach of even the most formidable Grey Robe, while the Ring of a Hundred Souls had been destroyed when the Witch-Queen was defeated. The battle would need to take place without the use of godly weapons. The powers of the darkness were disruptive and chaotic by nature. Even an average talisman housing the spirit of a single man of the darkness was difficult to tame. The light was more malleable and served its masters with subtle efficiency, if they have practiced their craft and developed their discipline over the years. The creation of talismans was forbidden amongst the practitioners of the light, except in the Wizarding Clans, because the removal of the soul from the body was a difficult and dangerous process.

The Grey Robes were the most undesirable of the Wizarding Clans because of their longtime affinity with the darkness in the Art. The Black Prince had always been their patron god but it was not until he appeared within the living world in the flesh that the Grey Robes openly turned on the other clans. The Wyt Robes were believed to be the most powerful of the clans by the general population and most the Grey Robes resented them for it. Some of the Greys remained in unison with the other clans despite being ejected from their brotherhood by their superiors who followed the Black Prince into battle. They turned their wands against their peers in the service of their fallen god and fractured their ancient fraternity. Those Grey Robes who yearned for peace escaped to Ikaria, seeking the protection of the Elfin Lady of the Green City.

"We will follow wherever you lead us, Gareth," said one of the brothers near the back of the great hall.

"Aye," echoed several voices.

"Then make ready for war," shouted Gareth.

"If you go to war now each and every one of you will die," said the voice of a woman, once the Greys had settled. The Grey Robes searched for the source of the disturbance, finding to their surprise that a group of five women had entered the great hall by way of the courtyard arches. Four of them were dressed in plain black robes with a single yellow rose embroidered on the chest. The other wore elegant purple robes stitched with silver and embroidered with pearls. Over her face, she wore a thin black veil that obscured her features but one could just make out the raven black color of her hair and the long curves of her pale face.

"What would monk-women know about such things?" barked Gareth, "Yes…I know who you are. You are those five holy sisters going from village to village converting the laypeople to the Temple of the One God…we are not laypeople, madam, and have no need of your god."

"All are in need of the True Mysteries," replied the veiled woman, "come my brother, let us speak alone…"

"I have nothing more to say," said Gareth.

"But I do," said the veiled woman.

Gareth never entertained the idea of converting to the Temple of the One God, not only because they discouraged the practice of the Art but because he was from an ancient bloodline of the Wizarding Clans. Gareth, the greatest acolyte of the Black Prince, believed his master would one day return and reclaim dominion over the world. The Black Prince was the god of the Grey Robes and the Greys were not looking to replace him. But there was something about this monk-woman that intrigued him. Perhaps it was the mystery of her identity or her forceful insistence that he listen. He signaled for her to follow him away from the great hall and down one of the many passageways leading to the other parts of the ruined palace.

"Say what you need to say and be quick about it woman," he said once they were comfortably out of earshot from those gathered in the hall.

"You seek power," she said, "and there is no greater power than that of the One God."

"And why is it you congregants believe the One God to be so strong? I have never seen or felt his power…"

"It's simple. The One God's power is now absolute. There are no other gods or goddesses still walking amongst us in Albion. They abandoned men long, long ago and took with them their influence over the world that exists here…"

"But the One God discourages the practice of magic," said Gareth.

"Wrong…the One God forbids practicing the light in the Art. They worship the Old Gods and draw their magic from an otherworldly source. The darkness in the Art has always come directly from the living world, from the fears and temptations existing within the human heart. That energy was focused behind the Black Prince but now he's gone."

Gareth was still suspicious of the veiled woman and her intentions but he knew part of what she had said to be true. Without the Black Prince, the power of the Grey Robes' wands would be diminished and weak.

"What is your name woman?" asked Gareth.

"I am called Faceless," she replied.

"And you can guarantee that, if we join your temple, we will have the power we need to destroy the Wyt Robes?"

"I can," she said.

"I believe we will take you up on your offer…we will follow the One God in both name and strength."

"I think that wise."

Gareth and Faceless returned to the great hall and stood on the raised plinth at the head of the others. The others were too busy bickering to notice that their leader had returned. It wasn't until Gareth took Faceless' hand in his and raised them high above his head that the four other monk-women broke out in jubilation, much to the confusion of the Grey Robes. The cheers in the hall died down as soon as they had erupted. The room fell into complete silence as everyone looked at their leaders.

"Brothers," shouted Gareth, "in order to weather this storm we must stand with our cousins in the Temple of the One God…we must allow our magic to combine with their prayers and perhaps we will have the strength to retake the throne…who's with me?"

"We will follow you always," said one of the brothers.

"Aye," confirmed the rest.

"Take up your wands in the name of the Blessed Father," added Faceless, "any crime you commit in this great time of need will be forgiven as you are washed clean in the sacred waters of the holy temple. Go forth in his hallowed name and bring down the usurpers who have stolen the crown for their long dead gods…"

"I agree, my brothers," said Gareth, "in solidarity with the Tetrarchs of the Golden Temple and these, their emissaries, their monk-women, their Divine Matriarchs."

Gareth didn't really believe in the One God, at least not in that moment. He saw the proposition posed by Faceless as a means to satisfy his lust for revenge. Once the Wyts were destroyed and the Eternal City secured, he had every intention of turning on the Tetrarchs and claiming the throne for the Grey Robes and the Black Prince. It is unclear whether Faceless was aware of his duplicity. She was the epitome of stoicism and her own intentions were a mystery. The partnership they formed that night worked better than either foresaw. The people at the heart of the Atland were resoundingly dedicated to the Old Religion but the outlands had already converted to the Temple of the One God, while the barbarians living beyond were followers of the darkness. The barbarians had served as Sellswords under the rule of the Black Prince and were more than willing to return to the service of the Grey Robes, provided the price was right.

The Wyt Robes were never offended by the presence of Tetrarchs in the Eternal City and allowed the congregants of the One God to come and go as they pleased, including the five women calling themselves the Divine Matriarchs. The constant flow of Tetrarchs and monks provided easy cover for the Grey Robes to infiltrate the city and establish a base of operations within the Temple of the One God in the fifth district. For nearly a month, the Greys quietly waited, watching the Wyts attempt to organize a theocratic government based around the ancestral traditions of the Old Religion. On the Night of the Winter Fires, when the city's inhabitants were gathered in the Palace of Silver Light to honor and appease the god of the frosts, the Grey Robes erupted into the streets in terrifying numbers to make war upon their enemies. A terrible storm formed above the Eternal City in the measure of a single breath, its black clouds belching forth acid rain that stung and reddened the flesh of all those it fell upon. There were great flashes of white and black light as the Wyts and Greys converged upon the streets in open battle. Some people thought fireworks were being lit in celebration of the festivities.

The forces of light and darkness fought for hours at a stalemate until the Grey Robes were joined by the followers of the One God, brandishing swords and spears, pitchforks and cutlery, urged into the streets by the Tetrarchs and monks and Divine Matriarchs. For unexplainable reasons, the magic of the Wyt Robes had no effect upon the followers of the One God. They were shielded by some invisible and powerful force. The congregants cut down every Wyt in their path with ruthless apathy, seizing the moment to fight for the glory of their faith. The Divine Matriarchs, led by Faceless, and Gareth overtook the Palace of Silver Light without opposition and watched the whole chaotic war unfold from the highest balcony upon the southern tower of the palace.

As the sun ascended over the eastern horizon, the few remaining Wyt Robes succeeded in storming the Palace of Silver Light, blowing the great western gate off the hinge with the power of their magic rings. They fought the followers of the One God gathered in the hallways and raced up the endless stair of the southern tower. They had seen Gareth standing upon the balcony. They believed if he was defeated the other Greys would lose their will to fight. The Wyts were led by the three greatest men of their clan: Braanos, Maglos, and Nestor. Each rushed into the viewing room where

Gareth and Faceless were gathered with a few Grey Robes and the other Divine Matriarchs. Nestor struck at Gareth directly, conjuring several violent bolts of electricity and hurtling them in Gareth's direction. Gareth deflected each after invoking an invisible shield. Braanos fought the other Greys and Maglos restrained the Matriarchs in the corner of the room.

"I should've known I'd find you here cowering in a corner," said Nestor as he hurtled a ball of green fire towards Gareth.

Gareth transmuted the fire into water which hurtled to the floor with an ear-deafening splash. They each conjured a bright sphere of light, one white, one black, which expanded outward until they crashed into one another, pushing back and forth like spoiled siblings fighting over the last piece of candy.

"We were always evenly matched, Nestor," sneered Gareth.

"I don't remember it that way. I remember you feeling inferior to the rest of us so much that you renounced your place in the ranks of our brotherhood to embrace a darker path."

"You would remember it that way," spat Gareth. He forced his sphere of black light to expand outward with such force that it caused the white light surrounding Nestor to shatter like a pane of broken glass. Meanwhile, Braanos was brought to his knees and disarmed of his ring by the other Grey Robes in the room, leaving only Maglos standing. Gareth conjured a sword out of thin air and swung it downward, meaning to decapitate Nestor, right there on the floor, with only the Grey Robes and Matriarchs as witnesses.

"STOP," commanded Faceless from beneath her black veil, "you must not kill him here...he should be made an example to the rest of the people who would defy the will of the One God."

Maglos took the opportunity to bring down Faceless but none of his magic was effective against her. She laughed slightly as she walked over to stand before him, pulling his ring from his finger and throwing it to the ground. Maglos stared through Faceless' veil with great intensity until at last a look of recognition adorned his face.

"I know you," he said. Faceless struck him on the back of the head with her fist, knocking him unconscious to the floor. He was dragged away in chains alongside Braanos and Nestor.

The following afternoon, when all the preparations were made, those last three Wyt Robes were marched into the courtyard of the Palace of Silver Light in their full ceremonial regalia. Each was tied to a separate stake with bundles of kindling piled at their feet while Gareth and the Matriarchs watched from the nearby royal stand, where once the Elfin Empresses had watched the first emissaries of men arrive in the Eternal City. When the fire was set and the Wyts had begun to burn, there was a violent tremor, shaking the palace to its foundation. Gareth conjured a protective shield, expecting a surprise attack from an enemy he had overlooked but the quaking died away after only seconds.

"Enjoy this victory," said Braanos, Maglos, and Nestor in unison, as though they were speaking with a single voice, *"there will soon come a day when twin souls will rise in the east and they…they will possess the power to rid the world of your darkness forever. We know who you are, deceiver…and we know what you've done."*

The words of the three Wyt Robes gave way to screams as they were slowly consumed by fire. The Matriarchs watched apathetically before addressing the noblemen forced to bear witness to the executions. The four lesser Matriarchs remained silent. Only the voice of Faceless filled the courtyard from beneath her veil.

"A new day has come," she said, "no longer shall you pray at the dark altars of false gods…the Old Religion is as dead as the gods it claims to serve…there is but One God and all here shall take up his worship. You will abide by the laws of the Temple and the Tetrarchs and you will be an example for the rest of the world. Go back to your homes, dispose of your heretical idols and make ready for the golden future that awaits you."

Faceless retired to her chambers after the busy events of the day but she did not remove her veil or her thick purple robes. She sat in a chair near the window and looked down at the courtyard as though overcome by sadness. With a heavy sigh, she produced an antique diamond amulet from the drawer of a nearby dresser and placed it around her neck. There came a loud knock on the door and one of the lesser Matriarchs entered. She was young and attractive but also afraid as she approached Faceless, her eyes focused on the wall behind where her leader was standing.

"The Greys are preparing to leave, my Lady," said the lesser Matriarch, "I think they mean to betray us…"

"I know they do," said Faceless. She rushed out of the room and down the passages of the palace until she came to where Gareth was standing with the other Grey Robes. They were dressed in traditional charcoal robes covered with black cloaks and carried provisions that could sustain them until they reached any destination they might seek. Faceless approached Gareth and grabbed him by the wrist, forcing him into the nearby citadel where a statue covered by a sheet had just been placed above a flat stone altar.

"You are lucky you are a lady and my ally," said Gareth, "or I would strike you dead where you stand."

"Ever the gentleman," replied Faceless, "I couldn't allow you to leave before kneeling at the feet of the One God and offering thanks for our most joyous victory."

"You don't mean to stop us?" asked Gareth.

"I mean only for you to honor the one responsible for all our recent successes. This is the very statue that traveled with our holy caravan from our home in Lemuria. Now it will rest here in the Royal Temple and serve as an idol for the entire world to follow."

Faceless pulled the sheet from the statue, exposing not the hard, bearded face of the One God, but the image of a tall and beautiful woman, her hair wild and unkempt and her eyes bearing the pupils of a snake. In her right hand she held a diamond amulet and in her left a crown of gold. The look on the statue's face was one of contempt and loathing, while her body was unclothed, exposing the breasts and chaste-parts in exquisite detail. Gareth looked from the statue to Faceless and then back again.

"This is not the One God," said Gareth, "this is that darkmoon goddess we call the Poisoner of the Well."

"She is called Tsira," snapped Faceless as the antique amulet slipped from beneath her robes, dangling innocently from her neck.

"Where did you get that?" asked Gareth violently.

"I wondered if you would recognize it," smiled Faceless.

"I would know that amulet anywhere…it is the talisman of the Black Prince…they told me it had been destroyed."

"It almost was…but I saved it from the fire."

Faceless stared lovingly at the amulet, fondling the chain with her fingers as though it were the most beautiful thing she had ever seen. Gareth saw her eyes light up beneath her veil, a twisted smile upon her face. He began to understand she was not at all what she seemed and he was struck by a sudden fear that caused him to shrink from her. She noticed his reaction which served to fuel her growing authoritarian presence.

"This amulet and I go way back," said Faceless, "it was mine before your Black Prince stole it…its power sings to me, it calls for release, to manifest a new world through me."

"What does any of this have to do with the Poisoner?" asked Gareth.

"She will serve as the new face of the One God," said Faceless, "kneel and give thanks, brother."

"She is the most hated enemy of the Black Prince, I cannot…"

"I said KNEEL!" screamed Faceless. Gareth fell to his knees from the force of her command, held there before the statue of the Nameless Goddess, unable to move or speak. Faceless came to stand beside him, pulling a long ceremonial knife from the deep folds of her robe.

"You shall be the first sacrifice," she said, running the blade across Gareth's throat. Blood spurt from the wound as his breath gave way to gurgles and rasps. He fell to the floor and, after only minutes, made no further sounds. As the purple orb of his soul materialized above his dead body, Faceless reached out and plucked it from the air, stashing it in the folds of her robes along with the knife...

The Collective

As Anaximander led the withered and frail Queen Nerys from the Palace of Silver Light after their epic battle the broken Ring of a Hundred Souls fell from the sky at his feet. He picked it up and tucked it into his satchel and didn't give it another thought for many years. The ring had been emptied of its magic when the souls trapped inside were set free by the hands of the Old Gods. It was little more than an heirloom to remind Anaximander of the glorious day when he alone defeated the dreaded Witch-Queen.

Anaximander didn't look upon the ring again until the war between the Wyt and Grey Robes, orchestrated by the *Divine Matriarchs* of the One God. He joined the Wyts on the streets of the Eternal City but his power was not at its fullest because he was nearing the end of his long life. He was practically helpless as the Grey Robes and followers of the One God cut down one Wyt after the next, not only ending their lives but stealing their souls. They were gathered together in a single radiant orb of golden energy, stored inside a chest kept in the chambers of the leader of the Matriarchs, a mysterious woman calling herself Faceless. Anaximander felt the deaths of his dear friends deeper than any other woe he'd ever experienced and resolved he would find a way to free the souls of the Wyt Robes and deliver them personally to the Golden City on the distant shores of the Otherworld.

Anaximander fought his way from the Eternal City after the extermination of the Wyts. He barely escaped with his life and carried himself meagerly to the Green City in Ikaria. The Elfin Lady Rheis attempted to console him but his will was shattered. He had defeated the Witch-Queen, helped the Wyt Robes exile the Black Prince into the void, and brought healing energy into the world for over a century but the malicious death of the Wyt Robes erased all the pride he felt in those accomplishments. He was drowned in his misery, like a man tangled in the line of an anchor, doomed to die in the depths of the sea.

"I know you're hurting, old friend, but you must let go of your grief, before it consumes you," said Rheis to Anaximander one morning many days after the fall of the Wyt Robes.

"Leave me be," replied Anaximander.

"I have left you alone for far too long," said Rheis, "I wished to give you time to deal with your sadness but the time has come for you to regain your strength and remember who you are…you are the Wandering Wizard, the Master of the Mists, and the only mortal to ever look upon the faces of the Old Gods. You still have a purpose here."

"I've lost my will to fight."

"Nonsense…you have been defeated, not by the Greys or the One God, but by your own fears. What is it that holds you down, Anax?"

"I know that the Wyt Robes are dead. Jarek, Jaavik, Daru, Vaden…Braanos, Maglos, and Nestor. They were some of my closest friends and they're worse than gone. Their souls are being held prisoner, denied entrance into the Otherworld, robbed of the right to be reborn into the living world. I cannot abide the thought of them being used by the Greys to achieve their foul and dishonest aims…"

Anaximander stopped midsentence as a light bulb lit up in his brain. He produced the broken Ring of a Hundred Souls from his satchel and gazed down at it without blinking. The Elfin Lady Rheis read his mind as she reached out and took the ring from him.

"The ring can't be remade," she said, "the ruby can be mended and the silver repaired but the souls within are gone…the ring is powerless, Anax, and it should stay that way."

"You're right, my Lady, it's hopeless," replied Anaximander, taking the ring back and stashing it in his satchel.

In truth, Anaximander was not willing to abandon the souls of his friends and believed the ring to be the solution. He labored for many nights under the cover of darkness to remake the band of true silver and reset the diamonds before turning his attention to the cracked ruby. He was eager to have the task completed and failed to realize that he had left a small flaw in the depths of the ruby. Overlooking his mistake, he believed the repairs to be perfect and slipped the ring on his finger. He performed the secret ritual to pull his soul from the oaken staff he had carried since returning from the Otherworld and placed it within the ring. At once he felt his power grow and his mind refocus. He fled from the Green City, hidden within the shadows, and returned to the Atland. He went to the hills beyond the Eternal City and watched from afar as the Divine Matriarchs murdered the Grey Robes, one by one, and took total control of Albion. Anaximander feared the mysterious power of the One God that prevented his followers from being harmed by the forces of magic. Even with his soul residing within the Ring of a Hundred Souls, it was alone and paled in comparison to the power the ring had once possessed. In his hesitation, the other Wizarding Clans were driven from their homes and into exile.

Anaximander decided at last that his day had come. He slipped into the city and made his way to the palace without being noticed. It wasn't until he was within the wide passages of the Palace of Silver Light that a dozen guards descended on him, their swords drawn and their hearts filled with the desire to kill. Anaximander made short work of them. He transmuted their swords into poisonous vipers that lunged for their throats, biting them until they were laying lifeless on the ground. Anaximander continued on until he came to the Great Hall. Faceless was sitting on the black throne of the Wyt Kings, with the Yellow Rose of the One God restored to its crown. Her face was covered by a thin black veil, obscuring her features and adding a mysticism to her presence, but Anaximander had the strange sensation they had met before.

"The Wandering Wizard approaches," said Faceless with a cold, hollow voice, "no doubt here to save the souls of his fallen friends."

"I will not leave until they are freed and you are dead," said Anaximander.

Anaximander threw of bolt of lightning at Faceless who deflected it by conjuring a protective shield of psychokinetic energy. Anaximander wished to determine the nature of his enemy and his suspicions had been resoundingly confirmed.

"I see you are familiar with the Art," said Anaximander.

"Familiar," sneered Faceless, "I created it."

She called forth a powerful gust of wind that lifted Anaximander from his feet and deposited him several yards away. He used the ring to call the shadows and used them to blind Faceless while he ran towards her like a jack rabbit hopping through a field. He jumped into the air and brought the staff he still carried down on the throne with the force of an axe cutting through wood. The oaken staff snapped as it split the black stone throne in two but Faceless was nowhere to be seen. She had dematerialized into the very shadows depriving her of her sight, reappearing behind Anaximander with a long dagger held aloft in her fist. She drove the blade into his back once, then twice as he fell to his knees in shock. As she drove the blade into the back of his neck, he caught sight of the chest containing the souls of the Wyt Robes, resting on the wall behind the throne. He coughed up blood and felt his heart beginning to slow but he gathered his strength and used the ring to break the lock on the chest and set the spirits free.

A great sphere of golden radiance rose into the air, like the morning sun peeking over the eastern horizon. It began to blink and flicker like a twinkling star as it moved to hover above the dying Anaximander. Anaximander fell flat on his back and wheezed. Blood was pouring into his lungs and he had no strength to heal himself. He thought his time had come to finally pass away as a spirit to the Land of the Dead and felt the warmth of fulfillment wash over him. Instead of crossing over, as it should have, the golden orb, a blending of the seven souls of the fallen Wyt Robes, was reluctant to abandon Anaximander.

"What are you waiting for?" wheezed Anaximander towards the golden orb, "you're free...go and join our kin in the Otherworld. I will be right behind you."

The golden orb responded by rushing downward and merging with the Ring of a Hundred Souls. The ring vibrated violently as it released a powerful burst of white light, driving Faceless away with its brilliance and securing Anaximander's safety. Anaximander fell into a coma as the ring healed his wounds, taken to the deepest places of his subconscious to rest. Anaximander saw himself as he existed in the living world, limited by a body of flesh. He was laying leisurely on a couch overlooking a mountain valley with a glassy mountain lake in the distance. He could feel a warm wind blowing gently across his face and opened his eyes to see he was not alone. The seven Wyt Robes were also present, each lounging on their own couch, some eating grapes, others drinking wine.

"What is the meaning of this?" asked Anaximander, "Have we arrived in the Golden City so soon?"

"We are not in the Otherworld," replied all seven Wyts in unison, *"we are inside the deep places of your mind."*

"How is that possible?"

"You were dying...and we saved you. We took up residence in the ring but it projected us here, inside of you. The ring's power is intact and our souls are within it, just like yours, but our minds have been brought here to abide within your flesh. Perhaps you can explain this mystery."

"I was sure I had repaired the ring."

"Clearly the process was not completed. But we mustn't worry...we are a part of you now and you'll never be alone again. The healing is nearly complete. It's time to wake up and retreat from this place."

Anaximander woke to find himself in the Great Hall of the Palace of Silver Light, Faceless lying unconscious nearby. He thought his experience with the Wyt Robes was nothing more than a fever dream until a terrible headache caused him to double over in pain as the other seven minds emerged from within him. He lost his sanity in that moment. His own consciousness was broken like a glass falling on a wooden floor from a high shelf. The other seven minds were not malevolent but they were no longer concerned with their individual morals and concerns. They had evolved into something more than a man, a collective of brilliant minds, learned in the highest secrets of the Art. Each had been formidable in his own right and together they would be unstoppable. The pieces of Anaximander's broken mind were sewn into the collective but they were not made whole. Governance of his body was given over to the blended minds of the Wyt Robes who always spoke as one. Yet, even as the collective regained their strength, they were overwhelmed by an insatiable emptiness, the kind that leaves the spirit hollow and the mind drowned in melancholy.

The collective withdrew from the Eternal City and made their way to the Norn Mountains, to a secret chamber hidden in the high passes of the razor-peaks, a place known only to Anaximander. They went to sleep after building a roaring fire and were once again carried off into that place at the heart of Anaximander's subconscious, with the couches and the lake. Anaximander was asleep on his couch, snoring softly, in a state of endless slumber. The seven Wyt Robes sat around a wooden table nearby, making plans for the future.

"*We must do something,*" said Braanos.

"*The emptiness will consume us,*" said Maglos.

"*It will eat away at our spirits until there is nothing left but ash,*" added Jaavik.

"*Is there no way to be complete?*" asked Daru.

"*We must add to our brilliance. We need more souls. The ring held 100 fallen warriors and a Nameless Goddess at the height of its power,*" said Jarek.

"The ring must be returned to its former glory," said Nestor, *"we need ninety-two more mortals and a god to make the power complete."*

"And where shall we gather these souls?" asked Vaden.

The seven Wyt Robes stared at each other in silence for what seemed like hours, their faces absent any emotion, their eyes lacking the light that once shined from within them. The surroundings remained silent and still as long as the Wyt Robes sat in contemplation.

"The Wizarding Clans will gather soon in Ikaria," said Braanos, *"we should visit them...perhaps they will lead us to the souls we seek."*

"But we must remain hidden," said Maglos.

"They must think we are Anaximander," said Nestor.

"At least until we have found what we seek," said Vaden.

"And what of the Elfin Lady Rheis? Surely she will seek to stop us," said Daru nervously.

"Anyone who stand in our way will face the same fate," said Jarek.

"We will destroy them," said Jaavik.

The Last of the Clans

After the total extermination of the Wyt Robes at the hands of the Divine Matriarchs, the Grandmasters of the wizarding clans gathered in the deep places of Ikaria to discuss the future of Albion. Once great in number, there were only two Grandmasters left from each of the clans. These men were tired and weary after the recent rise of the Divine Matriarchs, depriving them of their homes and driving them into exile. The Brown Robes, Vanegg Kartha and Oliphan Aramos, were the first to arrive, followed by the Green Robes, Accolon Draed and Cavin Emras. A few minutes later, the Red Robes, Xavin Areyas and Dareth Enores, and the Blue Robes, Varos Savrin and Andros Arnmar, joined the others. Together they journeyed to the nearby stone table, at the heart of the rainforest, where the rogue Grey Robes, Naevrim Tannis and Vaklar Kenmar, were waiting. These men were the greatest of their respective orders.

The Grandmasters of the Wizarding Clans had not come together in council since the days of the Elfin Empresses. After the rise of the Wyt Kings, they began to bicker amongst themselves as they vied for supremacy. The Red and Grey Robes were always envious of the power and prestige of the Wyt Robes while the Green and Blue Robes looked upon the Wyts as their leaders and friends. The Brown Robes, who had always held a close friendship with the Wyts, departed from the High Mountain at the heart of the Atland to live in Ikaria before the rise of the Divine Matriarchs. The fighting between the clans never erupted into open war but there were many times it seemed it would. The clans were especially volatile after the Grey Robes fell into darkness. The majority of the Greys embraced the dominion of their master, the fallen god called the Black Prince, but a few went rogue and chose to remain loosely united with the other clans. Naevrim Tannis and Vaklar Kenmar were the most outspoken of these rogues, facing off against the only Grandmaster of the traditional Greys, Gareth Haras. While the Greys of Gareth Haras were deeply distrusted by the other clans, those following Naevrim and Vaklar continued to be respected for their place within the bloodlines.

"Thank you for coming, brothers," said Naevrim the Grey to the others when they were seated around the Stone Table.

"Like we had a choice," said Dareth the Red.

"When the Elfin Lady calls we must come," added Andros the Blue, "Where is she?"

"She's not coming," said Vaklar the Grey, "she believes that we alone should decide the future or our kind…"

"And what are we to decide?" asked Accolon the Green, "Where best to hide? I don't know about you, brothers, but I'm tired of hiding…I'm ready to reclaim my home and my temple…to again raise the statue of our god above the gates of Tansapar."

"How can we hope to fight the armies of the One God without the Wyts?" interrupted Andros the Blue.

"There are no more Wyt Robes," said Cavin the Green, "as hard as it is for me to say this, we must learn how to live without them…we have to find the strength to go forward without them. It will be hard but I'm sure we can survive."

"Not necessarily," came a voice from the thicket behind the Stone Table. The Grandmasters turned to see Anaximander walking towards them, holding tight to his oak staff and breathing heavily. Instead of his usual dirty brown traveling robes, he was dressed in pristine and bright white robes embroidered with silver thread. He seemed more regal and less geriatric as he came to sit amongst the others.

"My Lord Anaximander. What a surprise," said Accolon the Green.

"I have come to give you hope," said Anaximander, "the living Wyt Robes may be dead but there is yet a way to revive their order."

"How?" replied a few of the Grandmasters at once.

"During my time amongst the Old Gods I learned many things," said Anaximander, "including the secret initiation rites of all the wizarding clans...I can create more Wyt Robes and restore the balance to your ranks."

"That is truly a blessing," said Andros the Blue.

"Yes, a blessing," echoed Cavin the Green.

"Should we revive the Wyts?" asked Naevrim the Grey, "or should we let nature take its course?"

"I agree with Naevrim, the Wyts are dead. We should let their order rest in peace and move on with our lives," said Xavin the Red.

"It seems as always we cannot come to an agreement," interjected Vanegg the Brown, "the Blue and Green Robes stand behind the Wyts, while the Red and Grey Robes stand apart. I suppose it will be up to we Browns to make the final decision."

"It seems so," replied Anaximander.

"This is not something we can take lightly," said Oliphan the Brown, "I recommend we adjourn for two days...Vanegg and I will return to our clan and decide amongst ourselves what course of action we should take then render our decision when next we meet."

The wizarding clans returned to their homes throughout Ikaria as the Brown Robes debated but Anaximander didn't wait for their decision. He left that same night and journeyed, by way of a strong wind, to the Atland, seeking out the last five males within the bloodline of the Wyt Robes. He brought them together, explaining to them the importance of their role in the coming days of Albion. He instructed them in the ways of the Art and taught them the secret initiation rite of the Wyts, giving each the knowledge to transfer their souls into moonstone rings that would serve as their talismans and greatest weapons.

For nearly a year, Anaximander taught his five apprentices while the wizarding clans were left to wonder about his intentions. Had he remained in Ikaria and waited for the judgment of the Brown Robes, he would've learned they voted to allow him to create new members of the Wyt Robes but he had shown them grave disrespect by circumventing their authority and going forward without their approval. When the Grandmasters met Anaximander again, they were outraged at his insolence and demanded he answer for disrespecting them.

"How dare you call us here after what you've done," said Xavin the Red angrily.

"We know what you did," added Naevrim the Grey.

"Where are these new Wyt Robes?" said Cavin the Green.

"You didn't bring them with you?" interrupted Andros the Blue.

"I thought it best for them to remain in the Atland for now," said Anaximander.

"And to whose authority do they answer?" asked Vaklar the Grey, "Have you actually made one of these upstarts a Grandmaster?"

"I am their Grandmaster," replied Anaximander.

"This is absurd," snapped Dareth the Red, "you were born a serf…you are not a member of the bloodlines and yet you have the audacity to sit here before us and name yourself the sole Grandmaster of the Wyts."

"Regardless of what you think of me, what's done is done," said Anaximander, "the Wyt Robes have been restored and we are in the perfect position to strike against those harlots who dare to call themselves divine. My Wyt Robes are already hidden in positions of power, masquerading as congregants of the One God. When the time is right, they will ensure the gates of the Eternal City are open so we may enter under the cover of night and bring swift war against the Matriarchs."

The wizarding clans were again brought to a draw. The Blues and Greens reluctantly agreed with Anaximander and the Reds and Greys spoke out against him. The Browns were left to make the final decision and chose to follow Anaximander's plan because it seemed to be a viable way for them to free Albion from the authority of the Matriarchs of the One God and return to their homes in the Atland.

The united clans set sail at once and, within a week, arrived in the Atland. They hid their progress from prying eyes with a spell of concealment and came unopposed to the gates of the Eternal City, left open by the five Wyt Robes as requested by Anaximander. Anaximander remained in the Green City in Ikaria with the Elfin Lady Rheis to prepare the island in case the wizarding clans should fail. The clans were numerous and stormed the streets in open rebellion. They conjured spells to bring terrible storms, filling the skies with black clouds and blocking the light of the sun. They brought the elementals of the four corners from the beyond to appear and stand at their side in their great campaign to retake the Eternal City in the name of the Old Gods. The clans showed their great skill and knowledge of the Art as Atlantis was broken under the strength of their spells and enchantments.

Despite their extraordinary power, they were no match for the massive armies of the One God and the extraordinary power of the magic amulet secretly in the possession of Faceless, leader of the Matriarchs. The armies cast the elementals from the living world with ruthless efficiency and quelled the many tumults brought by the wizards preventing the city's total destruction. From the balcony of her high tower, Faceless employed the power of the Amulet of the One God and brought the clans to their knees, tearing the soul from one then another before using them to raise their undead bodies in her service. Most the wizards fell but the Grandmasters were able to return to Ikaria, beleaguered and discouraged. They came to the palace of the Green City, expecting to see Rheis sitting on her throne in all her majesty. Instead, they were greeted by Anaximander, wearing golden robes and a crown of rosewood upon his brow. He watched the Grandmasters as they entered with narrow eyes and, as they moved to stand before him, they saw his looks changing from one face to the next, his eyes blazing with a hidden fire.

"What is the meaning of this?" demanded Vanegg the Brown, referring to Anaximander sitting on Rheis' throne.

"*We are now ruler here,*" said Anaximander with not one but hundreds of voices, pouring forth from his open mouth like wine from a broken bottle.

"What have you done with Rheis?" asked Naevrim the Grey.

"*We have done nothing with your elfin mistress,*" said Anaximander, "*as the sun rose this morning, her attendants found her chambers empty…she has moved beyond the boundaries of this world and she has taken her godly talisman with her.*"

The Grandmasters looked at each other in alarm. If it was true Rheis had departed the living world, Ikaria would be left without its potent spells of protection, left open to assaults from the Matriarchs and their armies.

"*Not to worry, brothers. We shall maintain the protection of Ikaria.*"

"You don't have the power," said Xavin the Red.

"*But we do. We possess a power greater than any other save that held by the Deceiver in the Atland.*"

Anaximander held out his hand to show the Grandmasters the ring on his finger. It was made from true silver and set with a ruby encircled by diamonds. The ruby was glowing with a soft crimson light and the diamonds sparkled like they were storing rays of sunlight within them. The Grandmasters were in awe as their faces were drained of all color.

"How?" uttered Vanegg the Brown, "the Ring of a Hundred Souls was destroyed when you defeated the Witch-Queen. We've all heard the stories of its destruction."

"*It was broken,*" said Anaximander, "*by the Old Gods…but as Anaximander left the Palace of Silver Light, it fell from the sky at his feet. He picked it up and took it with him on his journeys. Each day, he took it out and looked at it lovingly. Even broken, the ring called to him, singing its song of enticement. Anaximander decided to mend it. He cast many spells and wore himself out calling all our souls to the ring…his mind was broken, his body dying. We saved him and he saved us. Now we dwell within him, by way of the ring."*

The Grandmasters backed away from Anaximander but the power of the Ring of a Hundred Souls froze them in their steps. They fought against their bonds, muttering various spells under their breath, calling balls of fire and spheres of ice, rushing winds, and vines stretching down from the nearby trees but nothing succeeded in breaking them free from the power of the magic ring.

"We can't allow you to leave," said Anaximander, *"we need you to add to our brilliance…we yearn for more. The absence of the Nameless Goddess has left a wound from which the ring cannot heal. We hope that each of you will help to fill that fracture."*

Anaximander waved his hand like he was going to bow to the Grandmasters. The ruby of the Ring of a Hundred Souls burned with fiery red light and, one by one, the Grandmasters fell dead to the ground. First the Browns, then the Greens, the Reds and the Blues, and finally Vaklar Kenmar. As they fell, their various talismans were broken and the radiant orbs of their souls were laid bare, gathering together into a single glowing sphere that flew through the air to join with the ring. Anaximander shifted uneasily in his seat, as each new soul brought him pain. Only Naevrim the Grey remained standing amidst his fallen comrades.

"Don't be sad for us, Naevrim," said the voice of Vaklar from the mouth of Anaximander, *"we are better now than we ever were in life. We're free. We wish you could feel such joy but the others have decided to leave you in your earthly woes so that you can take a message to the Deceiver in the Atland. Tell her we are still alive, we have not forgotten what she has done, and…we are coming for her."*

As Naevrim fled from the palace at the heart of the Green City, Anaximander went to the bedchambers that had belonged to the Elfin Lady Rheis and stared into the mirror, glaring at himself with eyes as crimson as freshly spilled blood. His reflection rippled and churned like the surface of a pond disrupted by a pebble as the image of the Elfin Lady Rheis appeared on the other side of the glass. She looked fatigued and disheveled but held herself proudly and with poise.

"We have succeeded in bringing the Grandmasters into our collection," said Anaximander with nineteen voices, *"but we still hunger…what can we do to ease this pain, Lady?"*

"You expect me to help you?" sneered Rheis from her prison within the depths of the glass.

"You will if you expect to remain alive…you are in our world now and all we need do is wave a hand to strike you down and join you with us. Then we would know where you've hid the Autumn Crown…we would know how to ease our suffering…maybe we would find our Mother again."

"What's stopping you? If you think me to be such an asset than I should rightly be inside you."

"Perhaps its best for us to leave you alone in this prison for the rest of your long life as punishment for defying us."

"You want to know what I think. You can't bring me inside you, just as you couldn't touch the Autumn Crown. You are somehow allergic to the essence of Elfkind."

"You couldn't be more wrong, Lady. We are not allergic to elves, as you say, but we are eager to not bring you to harm if it can be helped. We've heard tell of a prophecy uttered by the Wyt Robes as they burned upon the pyre. They spoke of two souls that would possess the power within them to save this world from total annihilation. We believe these souls will come from the union of an elf and a man, the blending of the silver spirit and the golden. Only such a creature could have a power yet unseen in Albion…tell us, Rheis, have you ever laid with a man?"

"I have not and I never will."

"What of your kin…there were two other Elfkind walking in the living world after the disappearance of your people. One came to be called the Red Witch and fell when the Black Prince returned to power. The other has not been seen since…you wouldn't happen to know where she is?"

"I'm not telling you anything," spat Rheis as she turned to walk away into the background of her glassy prison.

"Don't walk away from us, Rheis," snapped Anaximander, reaching out and touching the glass. Rheis doubled over in pain as she was yanked off her feet and forced back to stand where she had been before her moment of defiance.

"I suppose we have no choice," continued Anaximander as he struck her down, joining her spirit with the Ring of a Hundred Souls while her body fell lifelessly into the depths of the mirror. As Rheis' soul merged with the others they were made aware of her most guarded secrets. They learned that the other elfin female was called Caenara and she was living in the depths of the Sylveroad Forest in the east of the Atland. They learned the location of the secret passages leading under the sea from Ikaria to the Ruined City. But they did not learn the location of the Autumn Crown. Rheis had given it into the care of a masked individual she never referred to by name. Anaximander left the safety of Ikaria that night to return to the Atland in search of the Lady Caenara…

Twin Souls

After returning to the living world from the Palace of the Dead, the Lady Rheis, the Lady Leanida, and the Lady Caenara were greeted by a world where the Elfkind no longer existed. The Lady Rheis was devastated, allowing her anger to dictate her future as she disappeared into the night, journeying to the Eternal City searching for answers and for revenge. The Lady Leanida thought first of the Amulet of the One God and went to the Red Tower at the edge of the Wynterlande Forest to take up its protection, leaving the Lady Caenara to question what she should do and where she should go now that her people were extinct.

She decided she would never again walk in her natural form under the light of the sun, using the power of the glamour to create a new human face for herself, a young and beautiful lady with freckled skin and bright red hair, tall and graceful and pleasing to look upon. The Atland was no longer safe for her but she was compelled to linger in the small villages in the outlying countryside, curious about what men had become, wondering at the fate of the future now that the Elfkind were no more. She had never been driven to supremacy like Rheis or devoted to her duties like Leanida. Above all, she desired a secluded home and a quiet life. She was skilled in the uses of the Art, known amongst her own kind as the Firebrand because of her natural affinity with fire. She never openly used her magic, instead pretending to be a follower of the One God. She created a backstory for herself and denied ever having lived in the Eternal City, hoping to fit into the world of men as a common woman.

Caenara was determined of two things: she would never reveal her true identity to another living soul and she would never fall in love with a man. She feared men and what might come of a union of the two species. Never before had a child of both Elfkind and Mankind walked the living world. It was forbidden by the ancestral caste system for the races to know one another carnally or to mix the bloodlines. Caenara knew it could be done. She had heard the stories of the Elfin Lady Luarra and her love of the man, Joran.

Joran was a prince of the outlands during the age of the Elfin Empresses while the Elfin Lady Luarra was a daughter of one of the late High Kings of Atlantis. Like Caenara, Luarra was skilled in the uses of the Art but desired above all to live her own life and love whom she chose, despite the objections of her controlling father. Luarra had always been drawn to men and, in one night of passion under the light of the full moon, she conceived a child with Joran. Joran was called before his father and stripped of his title, doomed to wander the world as a vagrant and hermit, while the Elfin Lady Luarra and her unborn child were put to death, serving as an example to the rest of the world, demonstrating what would become of anyone who defied the law of the Empresses.

The Lady Caenara knew interbreeding would no longer be an issue because the Elfkind were no longer around to impose their laws. She feared what would happen if a child elfin in appearance was born of a human couple. Man would put the baby to death and likely she and her lover as well. They would never abide the return of the Elfkind or their caste systems. She decided to settle in the deeps of the Sylveroad Woods on the eastern shores of the Atland, staying away from the villages at the edge of the forest. She stayed in seclusion for almost a hundred years. She missed the rise and fall of the Wyt Kings, the coming of the Witch-Queen, and the power of the Black Prince. It wasn't until the reign of the Wyt Robes that a young man came to the heart of the woods in search of the Boars of Ahtarrah.

The Boars of Ahtarrah were prized amongst the Uiwens because of their massive size. A single Boar of Ahtarrah could feed an entire Uiwen village for the whole winter but most Uiwen warrior hunters feared the Boars too much to actively pursue them.

The Boars were said to be the emissaries of Ahtarrah, the goddess of all woodland creatures and were sacred to the Elfkind. Caenara had communed with them many times. They were gentle creatures and feared little that dwelt in the heart of the forest. They ran only from men who disrespected the woodland goddess by preying upon her most honored creatures. Only the bravest of men dared to venture into the dominion of the Boars. Elam Anfa was one of them.

Elam Anfa was a member of the Atlandish Tribe called the Uiwens, a warrior clan renowned for their mastery of horses and their unique metalworks. Elam was the son of a chieftain, held in great honor amongst his peers but he had yet to choose a wife or father children. His own father was in the last days of his life. He needed the comfort of grandchildren but no matter how hard Elam tried, he couldn't bring himself to marry. He was not attracted to any of the women in their clan, finding them to be wholly unsatisfying to look upon.

Uiwen women were equal to their male counterparts in every way, allowed to take up the spear and devote their lives to the hunt, demonstrating their prowess in a clearly masculine way. They allowed their body hair to grow freely and cared nothing for dresses or makeup. They engaged in demonstrations of sportsmanship and held contests of strength regularly against the men of their villages. Most Uiwen men accepted the rough and hardy disposition of their women but Elam desired a woman with femininity and sex appeal. He craved a truly Atlandish woman who took the time to comb her hair and shave her body.

The Lady Caenara was bathing in the waters of a cool mountain stream flowing gently from the heart of the forest. When Elam emerged from the bushes, catching sight of her naked body, he was mesmerized by the beauty of her hairless skin and perky breasts.

"I'm so sorry, madam," he said apologetically.

"I'm afraid you've caught me at my bath," said Caenara.

"I can see that," replied Elam.

Caenara wanted to run away but she was frozen by the warm feelings boiling up from the deep places of her body. She stood there like a statue in the stream as Elam came to stand before her, pulling off his tunic and pants in the process. She was like a siren that had ensnaring him with her song. She kissed him passionately, no longer able to deny her need for companionship and soon they were lying naked in the shallows of the water locked in a passionate embrace. He pushed his manhood inside her gently.

"Am I hurting you?" he asked kindly as he rocked back and forth.

"No," she exclaimed.

His member felt good inside her and she hungered for more. She rose and fell again and again upon his tumescent manhood as he lost his seed inside her. He fell exhausted at her side and she stared at him as he slept, questioning what he would think if he saw the real her.

Caenara was so intent on reliving that moment she failed to notice that her monthlies had ceased. She allowed herself to go against every instinct and fell in love with a man but she was not prepared to face what was growing within her belly. The reality of her pregnancy didn't set in until nine weeks after her first tryst with Elam, the day he failed to meet her at the stream. She pondered how much she missed him and how he made her feel, realizing Elam had become a part of her. She knew in that moment she had a child growing within her. Her first thought was what Elam would think when he learned he had conceived a child with one of the Elfkind.

Elam had not come to the stream that day because his father, a Chieftain of the Uiwens, insisted he meet a young woman from a neighboring clan, hoping that Elam would take a liking to the woman and bring her to his bed. Elam had not spoken of his dalliances with Caenara. He feared she would be rejected because she was not a Uiwen. He met the young woman, whose name was Elian, but he didn't take to her. The following morning, he returned to the stream to find Caenara sullenly throwing pebbles into the water.

"Where were you?" she asked.

"I had to take care of something for my father," said Elam, "but it doesn't matter…the only things that matters is that I love you, Caenara, and I want you to be my wife."

"I'm with child," said Caenara suddenly.

"You're…"

"With child, at least through the first term."

Elam moved to sit next to Caenara, wrapping his arms around her, pulling her into his chest.

"You must become my wife," he said, "that child will be my heir, it must have both its parents in its life."

"I have to tell you something," said Caenara, "I'm not exactly like you."

"I know you're not a Uiwen," replied Elam, "it doesn't matter."

"This will matter," said Caenara, freeing herself from Elam's grip and standing, dropping her glamour to reveal her true elfin form.

"You're…you're…you're an elf," said Elam in a panic.

"*I am Elfkind,*" replied Caenara telepathically.

"But I thought all the elves were dead," said Elam, "Weren't they all killed by the Wyt King?"

"*They are me and I am them,*" said Caenara, "*and our child will be half Elfkind…can you live with that?*"

Elam stood from where he was sitting and began to back away, moving towards the distant bushes and the path beyond but he stopped before Caenara was out of sight. His knees were shaking and he turned as pale as the full moon. Despite his clear discomfort, he continued to stand there and stare at Caenara in amazement.

"Did you enchant me?" he asked, "Did you use your magic to make me love you? Tell me…"

"I would never," said Caenara out loud while resuming her human disguise, "magic cannot make you fall in love and I would never have used its power for this…I've been avoiding mankind since my people vanished. I never wanted this to happen and I fear what will become of my child when your father and his warriors see its halfelfin face."

Elam was comforted by the reappearance of the face he had come to love, almost forgetting all he had just seen. He rejoined Caenara and put his arms around her shoulders.

"We will face them together," he said, "I promise you I won't allow any harm to come to our child."

"Do you still want me as your wife?"

"Yes, if you'll still have me."

"I will," said Caenara.

Elam brought Caenara to his village that night and introduced her to his father, demanding he accept her despite not being a Uiwen. The Chieftain was surprisingly understanding and eventually warmed to Caenara's charms. The rest of the village accepted Caenara as the wife of their future leader as well. She was much loved for her kindness, as well as her willingness to participate in the traditions of the Uiwens, like the roasting of boars in charcoal pits and the consumption of raw deer organs. She was given daily doses of herbs and tonics from the village midwives working to ensure the health and wellbeing of her and her unborn child. They took care to make sure she was comfortable and given all the things she might need. She received exotic foods from far off places to eat and relaxed to nightly massages from her doting husband. Elam never revealed the truth of her identity and slowly developed a fascination with her magic. She told him stories of the first days of the Elfkind and he asked about the magic they had brought from the stars. He was interested in the founding of the Eternal City and the reigns of the Elfin Empresses but he never asked more about her past than he did about her wellbeing. He yearned for the coming of their long awaited child.

"I hear two heartbeats," said the midwife named Dora while examining Caenara early one morning.

"Mine and the baby's," replied Caenara.

"No, m'Lady," continued Dora, "I hear two heartbeats in your womb…you're going to have twins."

Preview of

Halfelfin

Book One of *"The Tales of Albion Trilogy"*

Preview of Halfelfin

Elam came limping into the room, slamming the door and bolting it firm. He rushed over to his wife and infant sons crouched in the corner. The sky outside was filled with clouds, lit every few seconds by flashes of lightning and powerful claps of thunder that frightened the boys and shook the house. In the distance, there were a great many fires burning, not bonfires or brushfires, but houses and storehouses, stables and shops. The whole edge of the city was aflame and many dark figures could be seen darting from burning building to burning building brandishing swords and spears. Elam took his wife in his arms and hugged her close.

"It won't be long now," said Elam softly into his wife's ear, "you need to do exactly what I say. Save yourself, Caenara. You know I can't run with my injured leg. You have to think about the boys now."

"I won't leave without you," cried Caenara.

"You must! I'm not impervious to your powers, especially the ones you must invoke tonight, but the boys are. You must get them to safety. Take them back to Ikaria. Rheis will protect you."

Just then there came a loud pounding on the door, like someone was using a sharp axe to chop through wood, before the lock gave way and more than a dozen invaders wearing the tunics of the One God rushed into the room, brandishing their longswords, forged in the style of the Xani Barbarians. Caenara sobbed as the men advanced forward, not from fear but because she knew what she must sacrifice in order to secure the safety of her children. The twins were in small weaved baskets at Caenara's feet while Elam stood between his family and the invaders. If he had not hurt his leg in a recent riding accident, he would've drawn his sword and fought. His skill with a sword was exemplary and he may have been able to defeat the advancing warriors. The leader of the invaders, a madman called Gruun, stared into Elam's face, a sinister grin adorning his weathered face. For a few moments, they stood there, locked in an endless stare, each attempting to intimidate the other into submission. Then Gruun raised his sword and lunged forward. Despite his injury, Elam was able to dodge Gruun's attack three times before he was finally caught hard in the shoulder by his enemy's sharp blade.

"Now, Caenara," pleaded Elam, "do it now…"

"*Stop,*" screamed Caenara, not out loud but directly into the heads of the invaders and her husband. Gruun became frozen in place, paralyzed by the powerful psychic command. But the effect was only momentary and no sooner had Caenara started to move towards her husband than Gruun started to struggle against the enchantment. Her first plan, the one which would've saved her husband's life had failed and now she would have no choice but to resort to a more permanent solution.

As she stepped towards the center of the room, Caenara took on a different look, seemingly transforming from a meek and meager woman into an otherworldly being whose presence was fearsome to behold. She stood taller than any of the men and her shadow stretched out to cover every corner of the room. Her eyes became the color of molten silver and her hair brightened to a fiery red but the most notable transformation took place in her face. It became white to the point of being gaunt and contorted into a grotesque alien shape, erasing all vestiges of humanity that had been present in her only moments before. Finally, the mark of the crescent moon adorned her brow and shined with the same silvery light emanating from her eyes.

"You come here with your swords and spears," said Caenara telepathically, *"bringing your violence and your hatred brandished like a righteous weapon against the innocent. You burn our homes in the name of your One God and spill our blood for mistresses who have only ever sought to deceive you. I name you the condemned...and command you to burn in the fires of your own creation, that the divine justice of Annatar strike you down and boil your flesh from your bones!!"*

As though they had been tied to a pyre above a stack of brambles, each of the invaders instantly burst into flames, screaming and flailing as they were consumed slowly by the enchanted fire. Caenara paid no attention to the invaders. Her attention was drawn to her husband, also painfully burning away. She rushed over to him and put her hands on what remained of his charred face, tears cascading down her once again human face.

"I am so sorry," she sobbed.

"You did what had to be done..."

Elam died while Caenara held his smoldering remains in her arms. After her tears had subsided, she picked up the baskets holding her sons, one in each hand, and rushed out of the cottage. There was no one alive in the fields outside the house. The invaders had retreated with their spoils of war after butchering the villagers. Caenara ran furlong towards a grove of trees in the distance which would provide her cover as she made her way towards the small longboat she kept docked in a hidden lagoon about three miles south. She was almost to the edge of the miniature forest when a bolt of crackling purple lightning struck the ground at her feet.

"Did you really think it would be that easy?" laughed a shrill voice Caenara had hoped to never hear again.

From the nearby bushes stepped a short and stout woman shrouded in a black cloak, her rotting face indistinguishable amidst the shadows cast by her long hood. She had withered hands with long, scaly fingers and yellowed nails which twisted grotesquely into curls. Caenara dropped the baskets carrying the twins on the ground and then turned around to face her new attacker. She began to grow taller, once again transforming into her alien form, but before the process was complete the shrouded woman laughed again.

"Oh, I don't think so," she cackled and, with a flick of her wrist, she caused the shadows cast by the trees to come to life, wrapping themselves around Caenara as though they were ropes meant to tie her to the ground. She struggled against their power but she couldn't transform and was unable to access the full might of her powers.

"Oh how I have longed for this moment," sneered the woman.

"I am glad I can be of service, Idris. Now tell me, where are your sisters?" asked Caenara, "I'm sure they're nearby...you four are never apart...are they skulking in the shadows? Too afraid to come out into the light and face me?"

"We are here," echoed three voices in unison from behind where Caenara was held prisoner by the shadows. Two of the three were identical to Idris, shrouded and cloaked with deformed hands, but the third was a tall and beautiful young woman with alabaster skin and platinum hair. She could've passed for a princess in some foreign court and all those who gazed upon her became intoxicated by her looks.

"Aneira, Oryne, and Jadzia," smiled Caenara, "now that the famed Shadow-Weavers are all here, we can begin."

Suddenly there was a great burst of white light, as though someone had ignited a lantern as bright as the sun itself, blinding the Shadow-Weavers and freeing Caenara from her bonds. She instantly transformed into her Elfkind self and took flight, soaring towards Jadzia, the sister who was not covered in shrouds, and attacked her head on, knocking her to the ground before raising her hands and causing a sword to appear from nowhere. This sword was shaped like a scimitar, a blade carried by the easterlings, but it was made entirely from crystal and glowed as though the moonlight had become trapped within it. Caenara brought the blade down swiftly but Jadzia had already recovered, throwing something that seemed to be sand formed by shadows into Caenara's face. Caenara stumbled backwards, clawing at her own eyes and screaming from the intense burning sensation induced by Jadzia's 'black sand'.

Meanwhile, the source of the burst of light became apparent as a man emerged from the forest, a wizard armed with a long willow staff and dressed in the robes of the Green Order.

"Koneth atar aska'ani," echoed the voice of the wizard, as though it were thunder barreling through a ravine, "You will bow before the power of the Gods of Light, fallen sisters…"

Another burst of pure white light erupted around the Shadow-Weavers, causing them to scream in agony, for creatures of the darkness cannot endure the pure rays of light magic. The Shadow-Weavers tried to retaliate but each time they sought to use dark magic they were subdued by the wizard. Jadzia continued to fight with Caenara but even she was soon brought to submission. The wizard joined Caenara, who looked at him like an old friend reappearing after many absent years, and together they rounded on the dark sisters, intimidating them with their powerful presence.

"Is conjuring the *pure light* the only trick you can employ, wizard," spat Jadzia, her sisters standing at her heel, "we can also play such games, if that is what you wish…"

The world seemed to completely fade away as a blanket of darkness erupted from the sisters, shrouding their surroundings and depriving both Caenara and the wizard of their ability to see.

"You think me afraid of the darkness?" laughed the wizard.

"Fear was not our objective," replied Jadzia alone, "we meant only to blind you...to keep you from seeing us move..."

"*No!*" screamed Caenara.

The wizard made quick work of the blanket of darkness, willing it away as if it were an unpleasant smell being carried on the wind. Oryne and Idris had already vanished and Jadzia and Aneira were bent over the basket containing baby Aras. It took the wizard only seconds to realize what Caenara already knew. Arad was gone. Caenara hurtled herself at the remaining Shadow-Weavers, the air around her charging with the same fires that she had used to defeat the soldiers of the One God. For the first time that night, Jadzia looked afraid, grabbing Aneira by the arm and running off towards the woods, vanishing into the shadows as though they had stepped around a corner and out of sight. Caenara made to pursue them but the wizard placed her under a freezing enchantment, preventing her from moving and causing her to revert to her human form.

"Let me go, Tamriel," she spat viciously.

"Pursuing the Shadow-Weavers would be suicide," replied Tamriel, lifting his spell and setting Caenara free.

"That may be," cursed Caenara, "but they shall not have my son...I made a promise...take Aras to Rheis and keep him safe."

Tamriel knew what Caenara would do next and he attempted to stop her with a holding spell but she was too quick, disappearing in a puff of crimson smoke. Tamriel sighed dramatically and for the first time, his advanced age and physical infirmities became apparent. He leaned heavily on his staff as he walked over and picked up the wicker basket holding Aras. He stared lovingly at the baby sleeping gently, completely unaware of the loss of his brother and mother.

"I'm so sorry little one," he said to the baby, "it seems after only six months in this world, your life has already descended into chaos…perhaps you *will* be the one to save us."

TO BE CONTINUED - - -

Glossary of Terms

Albion: the living world.

Atlandish Men: the men indigenous to the Atland. They are average in height, possess olive/high yellow skin, and because of their long tutelage under Elfkind, they are the greatest of all men in all the uses of the Art.

Atlantis: the Eternal City built by Elfkind at the heart of the Atland to serve as the royal capitol of Albion under the rule of the Elfin Empresses.

Avalon: the mystical place between the mists marking the boundary of Albion and the River Lethe at the edge of the Otherworld.

Beddlebern: village of the Dunmors in the outer groves of the Wynterlande Forest.

Blue Robes: wizards who serve the god of the Sea.

Brown Robes: wizards who serve the goddess of the mountains.

Divine Matriarchs: five religious leaders ruling Atlantis and Lemuria in the name of the One God.

Dunmors: particularly small Gnomish Men living in the Wynterlande Forest.

Easterling Men: the men indigenous to the Easterling Isles. They are tall and possess yellow/gray skin. They are familiar with the Art but prefer to rely on their skill as warriors and swordsmen.

Elfkind: a race of visitors who descended from the stars to teach men the ways of the Old Gods and the wisdom of the Art.

Elmaeth: the Silver City where the souls of the fallen Elfkind dwell in the Otherworld.

Elnurea: the Golden City where the souls of fallen men dwell in the Otherworld.

Frozenland: the northernmost point in Albion.

Faeries: elemental beings who dwelt in Avalon before mysteriously disappearing.

Gnomish Men: the men indigenous to the north, they possess pale skin and typically stand between three and five feet tall. They have no skill in the uses of the Art and prefer to live in highland forests.

Grey Robes: servants of the fallen god called the Black Prince, once known as the God of Twilight.

Ikaria: a tropical island in the Southern Sea.

Green Robes: wizards who serve the goddess of the groves.

Itheria: the Green City at the heart of the dense rainforest on the isle of Ikaria, ruled by the Elfin Lady Rheis, holder of the Autumn Crown.

Lemuria: a small island off the coast of the Easterling Isles, legendary birthplace of the Temple of the One God and home of the Supreme Tetrarch within his Golden Citadel.

Necromancy: the act of viciously ripping out the soul [which generally causes death] and then using it to control their undead body.

Norn Giants: indigenous to the cold north, they possess pale skin and typically stand around seven feet tall. They have no skill in the uses of the Art but are terrifying warriors with immense physical strength.

Red Robes: wizards who serve the god of fire.

Shadow-Weavers: the lieutenants of the Black Prince.

Spirit-Magic: the act of transferring a soul from the body into a talisman to hone and amplify magic.

Tansapar: the Ruined City in the east of the Atland.

Tetrarchs: the High Priests of the One God.

The Amulet of the One: an extraordinarily powerful talisman powered by the soul of the One God.

The Art: the spellcraft taught to man by the Elfkind.

The Atland: a small continent at the heart of Albion, home of the Eternal City of Atlantis.

The Autumn Crown: an immensely powerful talisman powered by the soul of an Elfin Empress.

The Black Prince: the fallen god, Ragnar, who held dominion over Albion for nearly thirty years after the fall of the Witch-Queen.

The Easterling Isles: highland islands in the far east of Albion.

The Elfin Empresses: seven empresses who built and ruled Atlantis in succession at the dawn of living memory.

The Ennis Isles: the dark isles where the doorway to the Void is hidden.

The Ferryman: boatman who ferries spirits across the River Lethe.

The Marshland Woods: a blackthorn forest growing amidst a treacherous bog with the Well of Shadows at his heart.

The Mists: the magical boundary existing between Albion and Avalon.

The Nameless Goddess: the fallen goddess, Tsira, condemned to the Well of Shadows by the Old Gods.

The Old Gods: the emissaries of the universe who came to Albion before the dawn of living memory.

The One God: the god, Theis, who was murdered by the Nameless Goddess.

The Otherworld: the realm of the dead.

The Palace of the Dead: home of the Old Gods in the Otherworld.

The Red Witch: the Elfin Sorceress Leanida.

The Ring of a Hundred Souls: created by the Wyt Robe Wizard, Theron Kalenti, powered by the souls of a hundred fallen men with the strength to rival the Autumn Crown and the Amulet of the One God.

The River Lethe: the magical boundary existing between Avalon and the Otherworld. Living beings who drink from the river lose all their memories while its depths is the place where the spirits of the damned are consigned until moving passed their fears and hatred.

The Sylveroad Woods: home of the Boars of Ahtarrah in the northeast of the Atland.

The Undead: corpses raised from their graves through the dark art known as necromancy.

The Wandering Wizard: Anaximander the Immortal, Master of the Mists and Traveler of the Nine Worlds.

The Well of Shadows: eternal prison of the Nameless Goddess.

The Witch-Queen: terrorized Albion with an undead army for nine years.

The Wizarding Clans: the Wyt, Grey, Red, Green, Brown, and Blue Robes.

The Wynterlande Forest: a large forest in the far northwest of the Atland.

The Wyt Kings: Theron Kalenti, ruler of Albion for nineteen years after the Elfin Empresses, followed by his son, Eathon Kalenti who was murdered by his wife, Queen Nerys.

The Xani Barbarians: godless warriors who live in the Wasteland beyond the Easterling Isles.

Uiwens: tribe of Atlandish men living as hunter-gatherers on the edge of the Sylveroad Woods.

Wynter Men: tribe of Atlandish men living remotely on the highland plane on the edge of the Wynterlande Forest.

Wyt Robes: wizards who serve the god of light.

R.J. Pommarane is proud to have been born and raised in Oregon, discovering the wondrous mysteries of nature at an early age by exploring the woods with his father's family. R.J. graduated from Portland State University in 2008 with a BA in English before going on to attain a MA in Education in 2011. Since then, he has devoted his time to the contemplation of his own resolute spirituality, particularly through the expression of the written word. The author of <u>The Body Chaotic</u>, R.J. currently resides in Portland, OR, with his life-partner, Kevin, and their two cats: Kritty and Shadow-Weaver.

The art of Heather Lewis is developed entirely from her years of creative pursuits and the depths of her imagination. She currently resides in the Pacific Northwest with her husband, Nathan, and three children. She is primarily a stay-at-home mother and wife but dedicates much of her time to her creative endeavors. Her art is inspired mostly by the people in her life and the magic to be found in the serenity of nature.